NEW YORK RE\
CLASSICS

THE WHITE BEAR
and THE REARGUARD

HENRIK PONTOPPIDAN (1857–1943) was born in Fredericia, Denmark, into a family with deep roots in the Lutheran church. He rebelled against the pious atmosphere of home by moving to Copenhagen and studying to be an engineer. In 1879, he abandoned those studies to become a schoolteacher, a journalist, and a fiction writer. His first novels, inspired by the ideas of the realist critic Georg Brandes, focused on social issues of country and village life, but increasingly his work took a psychological turn, culminating in what is widely regarded as his major novel, *A Fortunate Man*. He is also the author of *The Apothecary's Daughters*; *Emanuel, or Children of the Soil*; and *The Promised Land*. He was awarded the Nobel Prize in Literature in 1917.

PAUL LARKIN is a journalist, filmmaker, critic, and translator from the Danish and other Scandinavian languages. In 1997 *The Gap in the Mountain . . . Our Journey into Europe*, the six-part film series he wrote and directed as an independent production for RTÉ, won him the European Journalist of the Year Award (the overall award and the film director category). In 2008, he was awarded the Best International Director prize at the New York Independent Film and Video Festival for his Irish-language docudrama *Imeacht na nIarlaí* (The Flight of the Earls) starring Stephen Rea. His translation of Henrik Pontoppidan's *A Fortunate Man* and Martin Hansen's *The Liar* are also published by NYRB Classics. He lives in a Gaeltacht area of County Donegal, Ireland, where Irish is the predominant language of everyday use.

THE WHITE BEAR *and* THE REARGUARD

HENRIK PONTOPPIDAN

Translated from the Danish by

PAUL LARKIN

NEW YORK REVIEW BOOKS

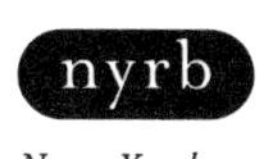

New York

THIS IS A NEW YORK REVIEW BOOK
PUBLISHED BY THE NEW YORK REVIEW OF BOOKS
207 East 32nd Street, New York, NY 10016
www.nyrb.com

Library of Congress Cataloging-in-Publication Data
Names: Pontoppidan, Henrik, 1857–1943, author. | Larkin, Paul, translator. |
Pontoppidan, Henrik, 1857–1943. Isbjørnen. English. | Pontoppidan, Henrik, 1857–1943. Nattevagt. English.
Title: White bear / by Henrik Pontoppidan; translated from the Danish by Paul Larkin.
Description: New York City: New York Review Books, 2025. | Series: New York Review Books classics |
Identifiers: LCCN 2024057867 (print) | LCCN 2024057868 (ebook) |
ISBN 9781681379296 (paperback) | ISBN 9781681379302 (ebook)
Subjects: LCGFT: Novels.
Classification: LCC PT8175.P6 I813 2025 (print) | LCC PT8175.P6 (ebook) |
DDC 839.813/72—dc23/eng/20241203
LC record available at https://lccn.loc.gov/2024057867
LC ebook record available at https://lccn.loc.gov/202

ISBN 978-1-68137-929-6
Available as an electronic book; ISBN 978-1-68137-930-2

The authorized representative in the EU for product safety and compliance is eucomply OÜ, Pärnu mnt 139b-14, 11317 Tallinn, Estonia, hello@eucompliancepartner.com, +33 757690241.

Printed in the United States of America on acid-free paper.
10 9 8 7 6 5 4 3 2 1

CONTENTS

THE WHITE BEAR

A Portrait

I

IMAGINE, dear reader, a large flame-red face, from which hangs a thick and matted snow-white beard. A mass of beard, indeed, where old soup and bread remnants also often reside, not to mention more bits of brown tobacco plug and snuff than is ever appetizing. Add to this a shining and gnarled forehead, bordered to the sides and back by white neck hairs hanging in curls over a coat collar; a pair of small, dense, furry ears; thick slabs of cottonwool-like eyebrows; and a mighty nose that tends to a bluish luster between large, penetrating, oceanic eyes. Add further to this countenance an incessant, seemingly unconscious animation; a frequent smile while in thought; an impish narrowing of one eye, along with a sudden, involuntary raising and lowering of those same weighty eyebrows, accompanied by similar movements of arm or shoulder—imagine all these features, and you will be able to form a rough image of the source of Uggelejre county seat's greatest distress; the anguish of its priests; the indignation of its schoolteachers, and the utter despair of the bishop himself—yes, this is the parish priest for Søby and Sorvad: one Thorkild Asger Ejnar Frederik Müller by name.

It can be further reported that Pastor Müller stood exactly six feet, three inches tall. That he had lost a finger on his left hand. And that regardless of summer or winter, he exhibited the same outlandish garb to the world, comprising a moth-eaten dogskin skullcap with earflaps, and a pair of gray-checkered trousers tucked into a pair of huge, sour-smelling boots. This odor emanating from the fish oil in which they were greased. This priest also wore a short hunter's jerkin that was shiny from severe overuse—a so-called cooler jacket—which was buttoned tightly around the girth of his mighty trunk. Not even in the most severe winter cold could he have been persuaded to change this attire. The only compromise he would make occurred in truly freezing weather, during which he would, it is true, tie his blue-and-white-striped cotton neckerchief around his throat, but otherwise he would just take an extra pinch of snuff from his pouch that was made of a seal's-bladder lining. This he always carried on his person and called his "heat bag."

Should it happen, in such inclement weather, that Pastor Müller encountered one of the local farming fraternity in the street, who tried to steal past him on the opposite footpath; said rustic displaying a dripping nose and runny eyes and half-congealed with the frost despite being swaddled in woolens—Pastor Müller would stop his own forward progress, produce his warmest smile, put his hands to his sides, and ignoring all formalities call out across the street: "Hello! You there! . . . For God's sake take care not to get frozen solid to your sheepskin coat, man!" After which Pastor Müller would continue his journey, but not without issuing a deafening laugh that shocked the very air for some distance around him and caused the two large, rangy dogs that always followed him to raise their snouts skywards and howl with wild abandon.

And the smile would remain there, beaming. His lips puckering and mouthing words in a most jovial fashion as he heeded his "life music"—the creaking sound of the snow under his boots. And always on the last hill, which overlooked the town, he would tarry for a while and straighten his bearlike limbs in order to fill his lungs with those ice-needle drafts of air, before stooping into the entrance of his once imposing rectory—Danish rectories and vicarages traditionally being points of architectural interest or even splendor in all towns and villages. Quite apart from also providing accommodation for the parish deacon, Pastor Müller's priestly abode had once housed a whole family and attendant servants. Now only a deacon remained, and he occupied some rooms on the upper floor.

Once inside, he was not received by the *de rigueur* diminutive priest's wife, ever ready with a warm embrace; who, still in her apron after setting a pie in the oven, would then relieve him of his sturdy walking stick and hat, brushing the snow off his coat, and stroking his wet cheek as she did so. Nor, therefore, by the little rectory "miss," running up to him in her bouncing pigtails, who would throw her arms around his neck, tug at his beard, and call him her "very naughty big and bold teddy bear!" The only thing to appear was an old, manky red cat that was returning from the attic with a rat in its half-open maw. The cat slipped into a large empty room that adjoined the corridor. A freshly slaughtered calf's carcass was suspended from the high ceiling in this room, its stomach entirely open and scoured, the better to cool it down as quickly as possible. Though this would not take long, as the ground floor was almost unheated.

Thus, we now better understand that, if Pastor Müller himself was a rare sight to behold for most townspeople, his dwelling—or "the hovel," as it was called by his parishioners—was viewed as no less an object of scandal. It was impossible to imagine anything that could be further removed from the cozy, carpeted priest's haven, with its plethora of small, tastefully arranged rooms lined with imposing bookshelves and comfy armchairs, in which our cosseted village priests are wont to potter, pulling on pipes as they ponder their sermons. For here, even in the priest's own living room, there was not so much as a rag over the window. The floor was as soiled and black as a newly turned field, and the spartan furniture—an old and cracked oilcloth sofa, a couple of small tables, an empty bookcase, and a decrepit wooden armchair with a leather backrest—was thrown around the room without the slightest heed paid to comfort and good order. The only thing that might pass for decoration was a peculiar collection of large bear and seal pelts, walrus teeth, and caribou antlers. These had been put up on one of the gable walls, as you might view such rarities in a museum. However even these "attractions" were not enough to offset the uninviting little table in the corner by the stove, which displayed a clay bowl containing the remains of a meat and vegetable soup concoction, a clump of hard rye bread, a wide jug that contained butter, or more probably lard, and a rough knife.

In other words, Søby's parish priest was a dedicated recluse and his whole existence was testimony to this. Or rather: his actual home was the whole region whose forests, heather-bedecked slopes, and upland heaths he roamed from morning to evening. And, armed as he was with either his rifle or his long oak-wood staff, he would invariably cause alarm among children and wayfaring people with his fierce appearance and reckless laughter.

Now, it is true that Pastor Müller, in his capacity as priest, was obliged to keep a wizened old biddy as a kind of housekeeper; an obligatory service that went with his professional position and state emolument. But the priest had declared war against her from his very first day there. Indeed, in his sheer obduracy, he would not even allow her to cook for him, let alone approach his living room. And he would otherwise erupt in furious rage on the few occasions when he suspected that this tentative and terrified old lady may have left a trace of herself in his inner sanctum.

On this particular day—and he in his most auspicious of winter moods—he strode into the rectory, then stopped for a moment on the threshold, as was his ingrained habit, to weigh the air and generally ascertain whether everything had been left untouched. Nothing untoward being traced there, he plunged his half-frozen fingers into his red sealskin snuff-pouch and took a decent portion in honor of the day. He then proceeded to prepare his usual hermit's supper. Such work consisted of throwing his bowl of soup remnants into the oven compartment in the stove. He then placed a pile of sticks on top of the slumbering embers in the firebox. Once the wood began to catch fire and the first savory aromas from the greasy soup bowl began to pervade the air, he rubbed his numbed hands with gleeful anticipation.

Suddenly a thought struck him. He went to a wall cupboard in the opposite corner, opened it with a mischievous smile, and extracted from its depths a paper-wrapped bottle, some of the contents of which he poured into two small colored glasses. These were on the dining table between the butter jug and the cob of bread. Then he knocked on the ceiling with something like the tusk of a narwhal, which he had hauled out from behind the sofa. That done, he let himself drop into the old armchair, which creaked and moaned under the weight of his huge body.

Directly above the living room, where Deacon Ruggaard had his rooms, the scrape of a chair could now be heard as it was being pushed back. Then footfall, softened by being ensconced in felt shoes, was heard across the floor up there—all the way to the opposite end of this large house, where it faded and was then accompanied by a creaking staircase. A number of doors were opened and closed throughout the otherwise empty rooms. Finally, there came a knock at Pastor Müller's own door.

Deacon Ruggaard was thirty years of age, portly of build, and with a face that smacked of a flat, newly licked greasy plate. Rather surprisingly for a religious who aspired to serious theology, he wore no beard. Here he stood now in the doorway, holding his gray housecoat tightly over his stomach bulge and looking questioningly at the armchair through his thick round spectacles.

"I believe," he said finally in a very broad Jutland dialect and pushing a wavering hand up to his glasses: "I believe that Pastor was knocking?"

"Yes yes . . . I was indeed!" The old warhorse jumped up theatrically, as if the thought had just had occurred to him. "It was just that . . . I just wanted to ask your High Reverence if you might not be tempted to join me in partaking of a wee dram . . . for medicinal purposes of course? I took the liberty of pouring you a small glass, sir . . . perhaps after one or two griddle cakes too many and you are feeling the pinch . . . for the digestion, you know . . . ?"

"Pastor Müller knows very well," the deacon interjected with barely concealed indignation, "he knows very well that I never ever indulge in alcohol or spirits outside of mealtimes. Really now, Pastor . . . it does strike me that this little comedy has become ancient. In fact and in truth, and if I may speak somewhat bluntly to my religious superior, I would most appreciate it if the Pastor would find some other ways of entertaining himself."

"Ah yes, yes, my apologies, yes . . ." sighed the old man, shaking his head, as if he knew shame. "But still and all and anyway . . . would

Your Reverence not care to enter a humble fellow priest's winter lair and share his epoch-making, dogmatic ponderings with his priest? If my intellectual better would only settle here for a while, I will fetch a bucket of coal and a footrest for you. Tell me again now... was it not pneumatology you were studying... the Holy Ghost and other higher spirits?... Anthropology also, was it not?... And how goes it with blessed—Petrus Lombardus, or Peter Lombard to us mere mortals?"

But Deacon Ruggaard remained standing in the doorway, looking down at this grizzled old ancient with an expression that shifted between pity and outrage.

"Pastor Müller seems to continually forget... almost deliberately forget, if I may say so... that he is my spiritual superior. The man to whom I am supposed to look for guidance and inspiration. So do you really think, Hr. Pastor, that it is appropriate for us to speak of these sacred things in such an offhand manner? It really does seem to me that, in these days when there are so many folk who are happy to mock and profane all things holy, that we religious should beware of being dragged down to their level of irreverence. I really do doubt that the good Pastor believes this to be the best way for us to pass our time, when out there among our flock there is so much ignorance and spiritual want. The very things that call most for our help! On that very point, I can report to Pastor that there was a message this afternoon that came in your absence from the wheelwright Hr. Povlsen from up near Sorvad Meadow, whose old father—as you may recall—is not long for this world. Well... it seems he is in a bad way and waiting his last in some distress and need. Pastor's carriage was not—as usual—roadworthy, but I promised to go across as soon as possible. But now the weather has turned for the worse and the roads are utterly impassable. And by the way, has Pastor been so good as to put my fur travel coat to one side for me? I've been searching for it these last few days and would be most grateful if Pastor could return it to me soonest."

"Dear Lord... is this poor man not right? Is he sick, or what?" the old man said to himself. His ponderings quite genuine. But then, immediately afterwards, he raised his head and a roguish smile once again played across his face.

"By the way, Your Bishopric... do you know what occurred to me today?"

"No, sir—I have not a notion what it might be."

"You should, I do believe by God, get married, Hr. Ruggaard!"

"Get married?... My word... what on earth do you mean, Hr. Pastor?"

"Yes, you see, my good man... I was only reading in the newspaper the other day about these newfangled stoves they've come up with—those transportable ones, you know. Now, what do you think... would you not think of marrying a yoke like that? It must surely be something for you! Transportable! Just imagine... you could walk at your leisure with it under your arm whenever you ventured out. And at night it would lie beside you and warm you in your bed... set the fire morning and evening, and there you have it, as it says in the advertisement! What do you say to that, Your Reverence? Isn't that a marvelous idea? Who needs fur travel coats..."

"Well... I really must entreat Hr. Pastor," the deacon interrupted him again, "to allow me back to my studies. I would sincerely be very grateful to him for that largesse"—bowing as he spoke as low as he could, with obvious ironic courtesy, and disappearing from the door.

Pastor Müller leaned back in his chair, firing a mighty salvo of laughter after the departing deacon for good measure. A thunderlaugh so loud that it shook moth and dust alike, made cobwebs tremble in the dark nooks and crannies of the room and the rats under the floorboards band together and prick up their ears. Up in the room above, the footsteps of the felt shoes and a chair being set aright could be heard. But the old man remained for some time, just sitting there and chuckling to himself, with outstretched legs and his hands folded over his quivering stomach.

All at once, he stood up. It was already dark. The gleam from the firebox in the stove fell across the two small glasses that stood untouched on the table. Without further ado, he grasped the first one in two of his huge fingers and emptied it. The contents of the other were quickly dispatched the same way.

Then he spun around, grabbed his staff from the corner, his cap from its hook—and was outside.

By now a full-blown snowstorm had developed. Pitch-black. A north-wind storm. The snow pelted from all sides and had already gathered in man-high drifts along the hedges and in every hollow. But the priest slammed his staff into the ground and hurled himself into this maelstrom. His dogs tagging closely by his side.

On the other side of the hills was an old man who was suffering. Expecting him and in need of him!

Back in "the hovel," meanwhile, the dust and cobwebs could once more settle back into place in the now becalmed atmosphere. In this new evening quiet, the rats stuck out their pointed snouts from their various holes in the dark corners; bolted across the floor; bit and chewed; squealed on hind legs and wriggled and tumbled over each other beneath the sofa. Just above them, the spiders, moths, and midges traversed the gable wall and its bearskins in silence, before moving on to the old cobwebs under the smoke-stained brown ceiling. And on the hot plate above the stove, the contents of the abandoned soup bowl gradually dried away to nothing but a sorry charred remnant.

It is the story of this priest, his life and fate in all its remarkable facets, that will now be related in what follows, dear reader.

Several generations ago there existed—and most likely still exists to this day—a royal decree, or ministerial statute, or something similar, pertaining to impoverished theological students. By way of this order, those would-be priests who were willing to commit to an unspecified period of time ministering to scattered flocks in the Danish colony of Greenland could receive an annual, and not insignificant, public stipend for the continuation of their studies and Christian good works, prior to departure. Truly, a charitable provision from those in power!

The remarkable thing was, that in a period of our recent history when theologians were otherwise in abundant supply, there were not many who answered this call. And those few who did rarely came from the top bracket. They were in fact, let the truth be said, mostly pathetic souls whose lives had already hit the rocks—desperate wretches who seized the state's proffered bait as a last lifeline when no other rescue was to be found.

The key issue in the statute was that the phrase "unspecified but lengthy period" to which a grantee committed himself extended over almost the entire remaining lifespan of said person. Only in exceptional cases could an earlier royal indulgence and permission to board a ship and travel home be expected.

Thus one better understands the trauma afflicting any young man who agreed to what, in effect, was lifelong exile. The trepidation he would suffer as he contemplated the day when his letter of summons would arrive; the ship would then put out to sea and the whole vista of his city or town, its spires and turrets, would gradually disappear beyond the endless waves rolling towards that coastline he nevermore would see. Or perhaps, if he were lucky, see again as a broken, gray-bearded old man, already made blind by the dazzle of endless snow and ice, after being buried alive up there in the terrible isolation of those eternal frozen wastes. Nor is it difficult to understand that these Greenland students, as these poor devils were called, with such daunting prospects ahead of them, did not always lead the most exemplary life in the short time they still had available to them in "civilization." The aforementioned precarious foothold on respectability—their previous misfortunes, disappointments, general lack and distress—had already rendered shaky the very ground under their feet. Then the desperate feeling of having sold their own souls soon killed off any last remnant of self-esteem. Thus they quickly descended into a misanthropic shadow world of notorious dives and drinking dens where they partook of life's pleasures with bestial voraciousness while there was still time... until one night they arrived back at their freezing-cold garret, and as they lit their taper candle did blanch to near fainting at the sight of that large blue letter; the official, ungainsayable summons to prepare for the theological examination in preparation for the first spring ship to that land of "the renunciation of sin, of the flesh, of the world, and the embrace of eternal ice," as it was called by the wretches so affected.

And in many regards, Thorkild Asger Ejnar Frederik Müller was much the same as this select group.

There may well still be those students who, from those bygone times, can remember a country scholar who was massive in size, but quiet and simple of disposition, and for which reasons provoked titters and laughter wherever he appeared. Those alumni who do remember him will most likely best recall the lectures in the theology auditorium, to which he had strayed a couple of times, but where his appearance immediately aroused such mirth and banter that he withdrew with haste ... or perhaps even better from one of those dingy and bleak student billiard rooms of that period. Here he would sit all day in the same dark corner with his elbows on his knees and his chin resting in his hands. As if his physical body were asleep, even as he gazed out at his friends around the billiard tables. The only signs of animation from him being the occasions when the corners of his mouth would be drawn to a dull smile. Perhaps after one of them accidentally spilled a glass of schnapps over his head, or executed some other prank at his expense. Without ever uttering words in response, or taking part in the merriment, but patiently tolerating being used as the butt of his comrades' random ridicule and jokes, he could sit for hours without moving—like some huge changeling in their midst. A ponderous and overly good-natured troll-being, who long ago had himself accepted the view of everyone else: that he had been born into this world as a freak.

In truth, there had also been unanimous, if much regretted, agreement on this point almost from the moment baby Thorkild first opened his large aqua-blue eyes in his mother's bedroom. Relatives and friends had not been slow, or quiet, in declaring that he was and would always be "abnormal." Preferring this more assuaging term to others that occurred to them about this monstrosity. And throughout his childhood, his poor worried mother was never done taking his big head between her hands and reminding him of how little he might expect from life. The burden Our Lord had placed on his shoulders must be borne with patience and humility.

Thorkild first saw the light of day in a small provincial town in North Jutland where his father was a teacher. However, he died shortly after the boy was born, leaving mother and child in much reduced circumstances. Thus, with financial help from some relatives, and under their strict supervision, he was placed in the town's grammar school from the age of ten. This being his dying father's greatest wish for his child. His surviving relatives, therefore, saw it as their duty to get him to the rank of student and onwards to university. There then followed many long and painful years for this unfortunate offspring. A grueling period in which his sponsors were several times on the verge of abandoning their educational efforts in despair. No doubt this was part of the reason that, when Thorkild—in his twentieth year—finally passed the university examination, he was immediately enrolled as a "Greenland student." The wider family by this stage having persuaded the weak and timid mother that there was no other path open for him.

Thorkild himself made no objections; reconciling himself to this decision with the same serenity with which he had gradually become accustomed to accepting all the vicissitudes that "fate" threw onto his broad back. And when the nature of the student locus into which he had been placed finally dawned on him, he duly followed the "Greenlanders" on their heels like the young beast-cub he was. In fact, to those very dens of iniquity and cellar dives already mentioned, but without apparently ever fully emerging from his own personal hibernation. In reality, however, he was neither as slow-witted nor as indifferent as he gave the appearance of being. The perennial calm he displayed in the face of all his humiliations was more in the nature of an innate grimace, behind which he had hidden since childhood. A screen for the sorrow and shame of being born such a wretched and useless human being. His indifference was a mask for the despair wrought from his highly refined instincts, which had sometimes brought him close to the thought and act of suicide in his most abject and lonely moments. But the thought of his mother was even stronger in the end and had always stayed his hand.

As for his physical appearance, it has to be said that a state of handsomeness never did finally arrive during his student days; neither in his own eyes, nor in those of others. A wild reddish beard sprang from his freckled face, and his stout limbs grew a further, ridiculous, mass. From day one, his fellow students had dubbed him "the big bear" and he really did put one in mind of such a creature when he was sitting among them, sunk in his half dozing state as he usually was—his big red paws and thumbs entwined at his mouth and his shaggy head propped onto his chest... for all the world a huge tamed bear; for whom, behind those half-closed eyes, the great forests and moorlands of his childhood ran in the obscure dreamscapes of his inner vision.

Thorkild's student days passed by and he at least had the benefits of his generous Greenland stipend, but fate once again intervened to decree that in those particular years an unusually harsh winter took the lives of two Danish priests in the northernmost part of Greenland, and on arriving back at his spartan loft room one evening he was confronted by the sight under his table lamp of the long before expected, but never really believed, "blue letter."

This was the first time in his life he experienced the very human trait of his legs giving way beneath him. For three whole days he stayed locked in his room without seeing another soul. A double-barreled cavalry pistol lay on the table beside him.

But during these torments a thought began to flicker ever brighter and brighter in his mind. A thought that rather shocked him in its ingeniousness. Shock, at the same time, that nobody had ever thought of such a simple thing before. For it now struck him very forcefully that it was impossible to make him a priest! For he had scarcely opened a book in the past five years and, ever since those vain attempts at entering the theology auditorium unnoticed, neither had he seen the insides of the university itself! He was completely empty of any priestly notion whatsoever... therefore... his reckonings told him that if he were to hand in all his written assignments for the examination completely unanswered, and did not utter a single word at his oral discussion and examination, then it would be impossible to award him any mark whatsoever—and consequently the authorities would have no choice but to allow him to remain in Denmark, at least in the short to medium term.

The time for the exam duly arrived and Thorkild stuck to his plan for the written tests without hesitation. A great outcry and cheering erupted among the student fraternity when the rumor spread that the written assignments submitted by the big Greenland bear were blank as the Arctic wasteland itself!

But alas and alack, Thorkild's reckonings had omitted the most important factor—the government ministry and the imprimatur of the royal crown therein embossed. In response to an approach from the Faculty of Theology, a ministerial reply was, in all confidence, issued to the effect that a way should be found for said candidate not only to pass the exam, but to do so in as timely a fashion as possible, so that this duly ordained man could be sent to the colonies with the first departing ship. It was, therefore, this remarkable train of events that led to the final comedy, which swiftly moved into the realm of legend at the university.

In front of an auditorium packed to the rafters with young and old clerics who had gathered to see this spectacle for themselves, poor Thorkild was forced to run a gauntlet of theology subjects, of which there were several and for which he could not even give a name. With a hand clamped on each knee and his eyes fixed at a spot on the floor—and feeling himself utterly preposterous in a borrowed black candidate's vestment—far too short in the arms and legs—he sat still and silent as a stone on his chair like a deaf-mute. Professors came and went. They raged. They twisted and turned like worms in their postures and exhortations, shook him by his shirt collar and roared into his ear... but not one syllable passed over his quivering lips.

Finally, in the very last subject, when the examiner—to almost universal jubilation in the auditorium—managed by a sudden ambush to extricate a "yes" to the question as to whether it was more than three centuries since Martin Luther lived, the process was brought to an end. Now he had given an answer! And now, bestowed with his testament of *Vix non contemnendus* (the barest minimum, short of *contemnent*—repudiation; his priest's diploma), and the strictest admonitions from the bishop himself to diligently and conscientiously recover all the ground he had so clearly and badly neglected, he was sent to the most northerly priestly vocation that existed anywhere in the whole world.

He was not even allowed to go home and take final leave of his mother. The ship was ready to sail and at anchor awaiting departure. So it was that, one afternoon in early April, that this very anchor was raised and Pastor Thorkild Müller was at sea and bound for Greenland.

Not a soul was there to bid him farewell. And very soon after, a wall of murk and fog veiled Denmark's coastline from his staring, disbelieving gaze.

2

BETWEEN two soaring headlands, at a place where the landmass rose ever skywards and the mountains—naked and black—jutted out into the very ice-filled sea itself, the arm of a fjord reached inwards to penetrate deep beyond the coastal landscape. At its mouth, the fjord was a wide bay, dotted with small snow-covered islands and skerries of bare rock, over which cruised thousands of snow-white birds. The air filled with their screams and cries. But gradually this winding inlet was forced into an ever-narrower defile by the flanking, utterly bare rockfaces whose steep sides gave way to mountains rising in peak after peak towards the heavens before disappearing into the clouds. But at its very base, the fjord widened again to form an almost circular lake, which filled the bottom of a mighty cauldron of scoured rock, whose more gentle slopes and crevices could support crowberry shrubs or moss-green and yellowish thickets. This sudden vegetation reflecting in the still waters at the bottom of the fjord.

It could sometimes happen during the short summer season—especially when a storm was imminent—that a whaling ship might find its way in here between the mountains. Its clanking anchor chains and human voices provoking echo all about . . . or that a whale from the great oceans beyond would go astray here, thrashing the waters among the skerries in vexation, until finally with column spouts and great noise it found its way out again. But otherwise, silence reigned here. Day and night. Deep and dormant beneath the noiseless fells and never broken . . . except in the height of summer and the days of the midnight sun when a music of sorts would emerge from the buzzing swarms of mosquitoes. Black dancing veils hovering over the gilded water, through which the sun's speckles were sifted. Every now and then a quick splash would sound out in the depths and a smooth black rump appear and disappear. Broad, snubby snouts would also suddenly break the water's surface to take in a fill of air. Then dive down again without a sound.

Down the mountainside comes the blue-gray arctic fox with its first drowsy steps. On a rock ledge it stops and yawns a red mouth... then shudders its fur and moves on... now it is trotting along the shoreline, where tiny gravel stones glisten in multicolored reflections from the shallow edge of the lake. The fox snaps lazily after a mosquito before rummaging through a pile of gnawed bones with its pointed snout. These are outside the entrance to an abandoned half-sunken cave dwelling, built from turf sods and stone. The fox then vanishes into its chill interior.

Indeed, scattered beneath overhanging cliff promontories—and embracing almost the whole circumference of this "lake" shoreline—was a veritable colony of similar sunken hollows—the miserable winter abodes of the indigenous people who otherwise preferred to live at the head of rivers and fjords along the exterior coastline. These cave dwellings were always readily abandoned at the first glimmer of spring and a modicum of sunshine. The whole camp would then head up to the caribou hunting grounds on the upland plains at the edge of the inland ice sheet. Also in this settlement was a most rudimentary stone chapel. This had been built hard up against the cliffside itself and had a wooden cross over the entrance. Perched just further up from this chapel on a mountain slope was a red-painted log cabin with white window frames, a timbered roof, and a fenced-off yard for the dogs. This was the rectory.

But this too was now abandoned. Apart that is from the fox, who would slip up there in the evenings—its fur full of mosquitos. There it would choose one of the corner posts, so as to scratch and rub itself.

But as the long winter nights approached and the snow began to settle over the land once again, life began to stir in this desolate crucible of stone. From the east, small pelt-clad figures worked their way down the mountain sides by way of husky, or sled-dog teams, which pulled their heavily laden sleds. Not all traveled by sled. Some came on skis—at breakneck speed across the slopes! Others arrived from the west, via the fjord, in large yellow umiak, sealskin boats, or in smaller kayaks . . . two, three families in floating groups, talking, squabbling, and laughing. The women pulled at the oars. Dark, ocher skin-tones and black-eyed. Some with still-suckling babies at their backs, ensconced inside a pouch at the upper back inside the expansive hood of the coat. A pouch these Inuit peoples called an *amaut*, part of the woman's baby-carrying coat called an *amauti*. And in every boat were piles of caribou and sealskins, lumps of blubber, cuts of bloody seal meat, game birds, stinking hides, and large pouches made of caribou bladders filled with mixtures of flour, grain, or peas, which had been bartered for some of their own wares at a trading post farther to the south.

Every new day saw additional families arriving at this seasonal colony. Utter silence was now replaced with noisy commotion around the lakeshore, made by people clad in furs and skins, who gave the impression of being still semi-intoxicated from the summer sun just passed and the excitement of the hunt up on the ice in the highland plains. The winter dwellings meanwhile had to be put in order. Stones, turf sods, and moss had to be gathered. The new skins had to be spread out over the rocks so as to be wind-dried. In remote, well-hidden crevices up in the mountains, the winter store was laid down inside stone dolmens and carefully covered with hides and packed snow. And in the damp darkness of the caves, the older women wandered around, talking aloud as they spread their skins over the sleeping-benches that were arranged in wall crevices and on suitable slabs of rock, filled the soapstone lamps with blubber oil, and hung the large cooking pots up under the low ceiling, which dripped with moisture.

And all the while, the sun sank farther and farther below the horizon and the murk flowed in from the north, accompanied by freezing snow showers and a biting ice-wind.

The long months of pitch-black winter night now reigned. The land entirely buried under fathom-high snowdrifts and the sea locked in ice-packs, and in such gloom that the eye saw nothing but dark contours all around. But for all this, signs of human life beneath this snow and ice mantle were still extant, no matter how faint. Here and there, a reddish gleam fell onto the snow-white blanket from a wall opening covered by skin and bladder membrane in the cave dwellings. The white blanket having receded and become lower due to the warmth emanating from belowground. Now and then, a bundle of fur and skin would creep out on all fours from the long, low path of flat stones that led out to the exterior. And as ever, the big, rangy dogs trotted around searching for scraps and howling at the bitterly cold night.

Far out on the frozen fjord itself, stiff-frozen fishermen stood watch at the breathing holes, from which seals would momentarily emerge for air. Like standing figures of ice, they stood there for hours, their harpoon at the ready and only moving their feet now and then so as to avoid freezing fast to the ice. Other figures moved out between the skerries with a bow and a sheaf of arrows, and others traveled even farther afield as winter supplies ran out and all fjords and bays became ice-locked.

And if hunger and general privation were often pressing towards the end of this season, they were seldom the cause of actual deaths. When the last piece of frozen blubber had been chewed and the soapstone lamp hanging from the low roof no longer burned due to a lack of sustenance, the people rolled up together on the stone benches and lay there in energy-saving silence. All waiting with wise endurance for the moment when the snow on the highest mountain peaks would be illuminated for the first time by that age-old golden glow. The still faint and pale but undoubted sign that the sun had broken through.

At which point, they would all come crawling out of their caves—large and small bundles of skin—rising on stiffened knees and staring with dull eyes up at the remarkable light, which—as if teasing them—appeared and then vanished on the mountain ridges up above. Old people and those so exhausted by hunger they could no longer stand were carried out into the open, so that they too could see how this gleam of promise edged and widened farther down the slopes day by day. Finally, the first slim and narrow but glowing sliver of sun peeked out over the blue-tinged mountains in the south. Big tears of joy ran down their hollowed cheeks. People shouted and clapped their hands. Jumped, as much as they could with their clumsy limbs, and fell on each other's necks in pure emotion. Mothers held up their children and cried out in pure rapture and, in imitation, the older children stretched out their small undernourished hands towards this all-powerful source of heat and threw their own voices into the hallelujah cacophony:

"*Seqineq! Seqineq!*—The Sun! The Sun!"

With every day that now passed, as the snow vanished in foaming streams down the mountain sides, the red ball of fire rose a little higher in the blue heavens and bestowed a tapestry of life, color, and warmth all over the land. And when at last the sun god never left the skies and day and night melded into one long sun-quivering day, cliffsides and crevices bloomed into broad swathes of glistening moss and reddish lichen; young shoots and plants that sprouted and anchored themselves as they proliferated; like an unruly, festive floral carpet across all slopes and in every valley. The berries from the crowberry bushes dared to peep forth; dwarf shrubs and thumb-sized arctic willow stems spread their tiny leaves and entrails ever outwards . . . all this explosion of life was echoed and reinforced by terrifying detonations all around the coast—blast upon blast—every time an iceberg broke loose from the fastland and set sail over the reopened sea.

Serene and majestic in their passage, these mighty navigators of the Arctic Ocean sailed onwards under the wine-colored sky . . . like fairy-tale castles . . . like floating crystal palaces, with high peaks and domed towers, sun-red, azure-blue, or as if dripping with blood and gold in their ever-changing reflections.

There was a great hubbub down by the lake. People were moving around in all haste at the water's edge and also hauling out those remaining scraps of pelts, skins, and bladder pouches they had not used up, or eaten the last of, during the winter. They had already gathered their fishing gear and packed it onto the kayak-shaped dogsleds. Or into the large yellow umiak boats used by the women. These had been beached in a row near the backshore.

The winter colony was breaking camp. Now that the sun had fully revealed itself, they hurried to their famed caribou hunt on the vast upland plains usually covered by ice and snow. Some of the caves had already been cleared and their inhabitants were at work on the high steppes. Those still below at the lakeshore had only one thought—to join their people in the ancient hunt.

On a bench outside the small log cabin that served as his rectory, Thorkild Müller was sitting gazing outwards. This elevated setting offered a grand view of life below. He sat in his accustomed forward-leaning position with his chin resting on his hands as he followed the frantic process of breaking camp that was unfolding at the lake-shore—the dogsleds being packed and lashed tight; the dogs harnessed; the weak and infirm being laid out on top of the bundles of pelts and hides. He himself was to spend the summer at the southern trading post a few miles to the south. The boat party which was to take him down the coast was due to arrive any day.

He had been sitting like that all day. Watching. Following with his eyes every family, as each in turn was—at last—finally ready for departure and with shouts of laughter and back and fro chat, began the arduous trek up over the rock faces and steep mossy slopes. Followed them each one. Until after several hours they were nothing more than small dark dots against the white mountain ridges. And then vanished. Even when they had disappeared, he had kept staring. As if the mountain had fallen away before his eyes, and beyond the slopes and peaks he could now survey the wide, suddenly lush high plains . . . see the *tupeq* tents erected in the lee of the high slopes. Their long wooden poles and striking sealskin covers at the entrance. Saw before him the pulses of smoke from the large campfire fueled by blubber oil, around which the dusky women sat encamped under the vast heavens. Saw the fleeing caribou with their bounding calves. The baying of the dogs. The halloos and shouts. As the mighty sun quivered above the soft, glistening, partially thawed muskeg terrain.

Then he had suddenly—in a rush of anxiety—averted his eyes, pushed his face down into his large freckled hands, and simply sat there. Gripped in great tides of emotion and inner turmoil.

He had endured a long and burdensome winter—this first winter. Night after interminable ice-bound night, he had been cooped in there. Sitting under that drowse-inducing oil lamp in that cramped and lonely room. Walled in by thick logs. His throbbing head clamped between his hands and reading reading reading—*Christianity and Paganism*; *Preaching Jesus amongst the Ungodly*; *Golden Treasures of Scripture*; *Common and Useful Methods for the Most Urgent Inculcation of Christian Doctrine*—and so it went on—text after text, Scripture after Scripture. A veritable war chest of evangelizing texts, which some Missionary Society members had "gifted" him on his journey to Greenland.

But no matter how much he had striven to bend his thoughts to what was demanded, it had been impossible for him to chain them to the books. With every sound that reached him from the lake down below, he had raised his great shaggy head to listen. And before he knew it, he was lost in guesses and surmises as to where the sound came from—was it the kayaks returning home from fishing? Or the folk flaying sealskins down at the beach? Or maybe the young people dancing their whirling, swinging pingasut folk dance in the moonlight in front of the caves? If he then heard the triumphant shouts he now knew so well, from the kayakers, as they did in fact enter the base of the fjord with a catch, it was impossible for him to contain his excitement any longer. He simply had to go out and see what was going on and what, exactly, was being brought home.

There were times when he had roused himself from a reverie, after realizing he had been standing for hours outside his door gazing out. Following the fervor and tension that arose in the bloody hunt for seals as they appeared on rock outcrops or ice floes. The stealth and expertise that was needed to club the seal so as not to damage the rest of the pelt. Or the furious pursuit of a bear that had been shot . . . a passion akin to his own boyhood vehemence—the source of so much grief for his poor mother and the disgust of his relatives—with the subsequent strictures and punishment to follow. One early morning some days beforehand, he had been walking briskly along the shoreline, lost in thought and in one of the more remote parts of the settlement. He had stopped abruptly to catch his breath and in the very same instance spotted a seal sunning itself on a bobbing ice floe, which was quite close to the shoreline. Suddenly gripped by some irresistible instinct, he had crawled on all fours behind a boulder and then begun to scrape the small stones beneath his feet, and at the same time whistle softly. Just as he had seen the native people do. And lo and behold . . . the seal began to cock its head to listen and then look around. Then it slipped its body off the floe and flopped into the water. Moments later, its large round head broke water, now closer to land. The seal now clearly listening again. His heart now thumping, he scuffed at the stones again and emitted another series of soft, lengthy whistles. The animal stuck its wide, bristle-filled snout in the air. Its nostrils flaring. Then it disappeared again. Only to reappear a third time, and now quite near to land. Thorkild crept farther forward and with all the might of his great arm fired a fist-sized, sharp-edged stone at its exposed head. The stone smacked dead center into its forehead. The water all around it bubbled red as the beast sank. In an instant, his hot sense of self-shame bestirred him. And tortured now by his curse of heathen savagery he went home and tried to bury himself once more under his mountain of books.

Very often in this period, his paternal grandfather came readily to his mind. A man he had never seen or met, but whose many gripping stories—full of terrifying and audacious adventures—had been recounted to him as a child. Back then, he had formed the impression that his grandfather had been a notorious poacher who dwelled, like a half-savage, deep in the heart of the vast Rold Forest in North Jutland, which was not far from Thorkild's birthplace. With its dense tree cover, changing landscape, and secluded pathways, the forest was an age-old haven for highwaymen and brigands. As he grew up, Thorkild's grandfather fired his imagination—as a hulking giant with a wild, red beard. This vision and its attendant legends were vivified further by the fact that his mother never ever mentioned him. Confirmation, therefore, of the shame his whole family felt at having such an inglorious antecedent. Only once had he heard his mother mention this ogre's name. And this was with a memorable expression his mother used when, in one of her more fretful and anxious phases, she had bemoaned the fact that he—Thorkild—was "just like him." He could still recall the mix of terror and elation his mother's words had provoked in his heart.

Thorkild raised his head, roused by the sound of voices from the path at the side of the mountain slope that led up to his home. Not long afterward, two pelt-clad figures appeared—an old man and a young woman—in whom he recognized old Ephraim and his daughter Rebecca—or Seqineq (Sun), as she was called, because of her welcoming appearance. Barking huskies down at the shore reminded him that they had come to bid farewell. Their dogs yapping in excitement now they sensed that departure across the fells was nigh.

Ephraim was small of build and old age had stooped him considerably. He had a long dark-brown face, whose only boast was a pair of unusually thick eyebrows and a set of well-preserved teeth. His eyes showed through what were little more than two slightly crooked incision lines wedged into his eyebrows. His nose was so flat that it could have been a random patch of skin thrown between his broad, bony cheekbones.

In his younger days, Ephraim had been one of the most daring hunters and fishermen in the whole colony and, even in his advanced years, he was still regarded as being someone who took his role as family provider very seriously. But the severe winters in the last few years had taken a heavy toll on him. Just like so many others, in a desperate search for nourishment, he had sometimes been forced to turn to seaweed and old fish heads, which he had dug up from the kitchen middens buried under the snow. He looked weak and afflicted.

Thorkild bade him be seated, after which the old man began to talk about his travel preparations and his hopes for what they might get done in the short summer season. He and his daughter were setting off along with some other families with whom they had shared a winter home. Therefore, as soon as the dogs had been fed, they would break camp that very hour to get across the first peaks before nightfall, such as it was. Thorkild, who still struggled with much of their indigenous Inuit language, listened rather distractedly to him. Rather, his attention was continuously pulled to Ephraim's daughter, Rebecca, or Seqineq. She stood against a boulder some distance from them, and from here sent stolen glances at this strangely shy and reticent priest. A man whom none of her people could fathom. When their eyes by chance met, they both colored and sought somewhere else to look.

Seqineq was a small, full-figured girl of eighteen years who had a somewhat lighter complexion than her father's. Another contrast was the brilliant life-lust that shone in her compact, angular eyes. Her pelt had been dyed with a red pigment and—draped closely around her pert, vigorous body as it was—suited her very well. Her "top"—as she called it—of straight, blue-black hair was tied just above her head with a gaudy decorated band of sealskin, and on her feet she wore a pair of brand-new sealskin bootees with white embroidery. She had clearly dressed up in honor of visiting the priest.

Finally, Ephraim stood up and took his leave. Thorkild shook both their proffered hands, but in such a hesitant, fraught, and distracted way that father and daughter looked at each other in puzzlement. And when they had gone, Thorkild stood in his doorway. His eyes following their every step as they negotiated the steep path. At a bend on the way down, Seqineq turned to look back for him. And at every bend thereafter, she turned again to see if he still stood there.

Thorkild's heart thumped against his chest. His blood banging in his head. For a few minutes he stood rooted there. His hand gripped around the doorframe as he battled with himself and his surging emotions. All at once, he took a few steps forward, put his great hands to his mouth, and shouted in a trembling voice:

"Ephraim! . . . Ephraim!"

Down below, at the very foot of the path, the two small shapes turned around.

"*Palase*! . . . Ai?" "Priest! . . . What is it?" the little man cried.

Towards evening of the same day, a few of the people who were to sail Thorkild down to the trading post arrived to help him carry his possessions to the boat. To their dismay, they found the house empty, the door closed, and the windows nailed down.

The priest had taken to the mountains with Ephraim and his entourage.

Thorkild was one of the first to return as the summer ended and the snow arrived again. Racing down and across the mountainsides on his skis, his dogs following him at a loping canter. Those who had not seen him since the previous spring would barely recognize him. Not only was his head now proud and raised, his eyes had come alive and his cheeks were flushed with color. However, the more discerning observers would also notice that the infinite gaze of the unending high plains now gleamed from his eyes. And there was an echo of the wild hunter's resounding halloo in the booming bark of his now quick-fire speech.

He was a man born anew... a rejuvenated soul. As he now constantly moved about in his new nomadic life, he himself noticed how fresh life sources had risen up within his inner self. Very often he was not even sure of his final destination in these wanderings, or who might be accompanying him from one trek to the next. One moment with this group or clan, the next with an entirely different group. In this way, he gradually came to know these people, their myriad ways, and their Kalaallisut, or perhaps the northern Inuktun language variant, most intimately. Tumbling and wrestling with the catch in the salmon races, or while hunting under the sparkling upland ice sheet. He even dared to become something of a leader up in these heights with Ephraim and his sons in order to hunt a caribou herd whose tracks and trail he himself had discovered. And once these indigenous people fully realized the true cut of their new priest, it was not long before they regarded him as one of their own. Had he not slept alongside them in their pelt-clad *tupeq* tents, between the women and children, a bearskin over him and a bundle of hides under his head? Had he not eaten along with them? Partaking of their vast pots of stew and other native fare—caribou meat cuts, cranberries cooked in lard, eider duck eggs, and, above all else, the summer's most celebrated meal: the large stuffed caribou intestines, with their original contents of half-digested plant food and drool still retained. And though some of the wider tribe were already skilled in firearms, as part of his gift back to them, he taught them how to shoot with the old rifle he had brought with him from Copenhagen. And when each long day drew to a close, and people sat encamped around the fire with its distinctive smell of seal or whale oil, he gave more of his own wealth to them by way of entertainment, as he recounted the legends and wild, dangerous adventures he remembered from his boyhood years. His audience betimes open-mouthed and listening with bated breath.

And once this man of the Danish cloth—the physical representative of Denmark's *imperium* in Greenland—had shed his skin and dared to leap, there was no going back. He who once was "Pastor Müller" closed his eyes and stopped up his ears to signs and noises of conscience. He simply let go, then drifted, drifted ... away from all that.

Even before winter had once more frozen the fjord and closed the sea straits, he had learned to steer a kayak and throw a harpoon with accuracy. Learned also to skewer a pheasant in flight with a smaller harpoon thrown from that same kayak. In fact, he became so adept that, back on land, he could hit a leaping hare from some distance. Time raced on unheeded out there among the skerries and rock islands during the *utoq* hunt—the season when the seals would lie prone on the surface of ice floes and rocks and a harpoon or rifle was used. Next, he could be in a sled with sixteen howling dogs in harness ... and they could be days up and down and over the mountains after the fox! Indeed, there were moments when he was just inside his own door late in the evening after an arduous expedition; had barely lain down under his pelt blanket in his bed when there was a knock at this window.

"What is it?"

"A bear! There's a bear out in the fjord, Priest!"

"Hoop-la!—A bear?"...The rifle down from the wall. His pelts back on. And into the night yet again.

—And he drifted and drifted.

It is true that there would be times when his wild surges of blood subsided for a moment, when he, as it were, came to observe his own face—and looked away. He would then become almost afraid of himself...the sight of his own hand, still bloody from helping with the flaying of seals. Or his uncut, unkempt beard. The suddenly alien sound of his deep voice. Unbidden, visions of his grandfather's terrifying aura would visit him. And the mute silence the name of this "ogre" invoked. The petrified stare in his mother's anxious eyes on the only occasion she had allowed his grandfather's name to pass her lips.

It was in just such a reflective mood that he was sitting one evening outside his door, his head between his hands. Fluctuating between nothing more than rueful thoughts and downright repentance. He had not maintained his priestly vows. Rather than converting and edifying heathens, they had converted him. Was this some latent savagery in his own bloodline that had welled up again through an inherited failing in his own character? The very unspoken indictment that had hung over him through all his days. Bone-weary and ready to drop, he had returned home from the outermost skerries, where a giant whale had stranded the day before and had since been brought ashore. This event had roused every man in the colony to action, so as to secure their own share of the spoils. Thorkild had, with his usual zeal, taken part in the retrieval of the carcass, and had then overseen both the dismemberment of this great beast and the distribution between all the participants. After moving among all the gore and florid chunks of bloody whale meat for a whole day, he now saw nothing but red before his eyes.

High over his head, the dark-blue sky was a vast vault studded with a myriad of gilt-edged stars. Far in the east, the moon rose in slow majesty over the mountain ridges, bestowing a singular milky glow all across the newly fallen snow. Every now and then the northern lights would appear as gigantic shimmering drapes in the sky.

Down by the lakeshore, where the seal-gut covers over the windows of the cave dwellings spilled luminous dots of red out across all that whiteness, loud calls, merriment, and song could be heard—testament to the unexpected bounty bestowed upon the colony by the capture of such a huge whale. Bustling, semi-dark pelt-bundles crawled in and out of their abodes. Even the dogs frolicked with joy.

Of a sudden, Thorkild heard footsteps very near to him.

He looked up. And there, in the path just above him—bathed in moonlight—was Seqineq... she laughed as she looked down at him. She was dressed in a traditional gleaming-white all-in-one anorak, which boasted black dogskin edging at the collar and wrists and more decoration in red bands. Her bright sealskin breeches were also adorned with red embroidery at the front. This matched her sealskin bootees, which were also dyed red. All these embellishments were literally topped by a gold-inlaid band that crowned her hair.

He gazed at her for some time. As if shaken from a dream. Her white teeth glistened in the moonlight, which spectral light lent a greenish sheen to her petite eyes.

"But... Is it you, dear?!"

Yes, of course it was her! She laughed her dry, staccato laughter and tugged at his beard. Did he not hear her coming up the path?

"But... my sweet girl!... You are so fine! All dressed up so splendidly!... Come... sit here!"

No, no, she could not stay today. She just came to bring her regards and tell him that her father had caught some ulk fish. So if he wanted some delicious soup, her mother was busy at the pot right at that moment!

"Ulk fish soup?... Your father has caught some ulk fish?"

Yes, he certainly had! But he needed to hurry up, because they were waiting for him. And paying no heed to the objections he began to make, she went directly into his living room and extinguished the oil lamp that was burning in there, illuminating an opened but dust-ridden book on the table. She then closed his door, and held her hand out to him, smiling.

But instead of immediately following her, Thorkild drew her to him by main force, took her head in his hands and, tilting it backwards, plumped one, two, three wildman kisses upon her mouth.

She was, of course, taken aback by these impromptu voracious caresses, but as she now lay there in his arms and looked up at him, a quiet jubilation danced in her eyes.

Down at the entrance to Ephraim's cave dwelling, the many deep footprints in the snow alone revealed that something unusual was taking place inside there. The ice-covered walls of the long, low entrance were also quite shiny from the many stiff sealskin garments that had pushed themselves through during the day, people being almost on all fours at the end of the corridor where a low door had to be pushed open to gain entry to the living quarters. The cramped conditions notwithstanding, the subterranean interior was packed with people—mainly members of the three families who lived there. These people were sitting, or lying down, on the benches that lined the dripping rock walls: men, women, and children alike—all seminaked due to the terrible heat and belching smoke that pervaded the interior atmosphere.

Standing and working at a large pot was an old, fat, and quite bald woman with bandy legs, her flaccid loins barely covered by a sealskin rag. The pot was suspended over the fire in the middle of the room, which was fueled by seal oil, and the woman was blackened with the smoke-grime thereof and by the general filth all about. A group of quiet children were sitting in one corner, eagerly chewing at meat bones, the grease dripping down their fingers.

They had given up waiting for the priest before starting. Everyone had taken fish from the pot with their fingers and now sat or lay and cut it into pieces with their knives. The cave now full of competing noises. All the chat and slurping mouths blending with the steam rising from the brown bodies, suddenly illuminated and then dimmed again as the flames from the flickering fire threw their light around the room.

At last, shuffling and scraping noises from outside were heard and Thorkild's familiar ringing "Halloo" burst forth at the entrance as he crawled through. The door was shoved open, and with lively greetings from all the bench occupants, he stooped into the cave—Seqineq slipped in behind his back. Thorkild removed his pelt coat and jerkin, stroked his hair, which was sweaty and unkempt, and then immediately inspected the fish, which the old woman pulled up from the simmering pot with her blackened fingers.

By now Seqineq had chosen a place. Deep in the cave's darkest recess. She was sitting low and crouched at her ease on her heels. Semi-naked herself now, with only a pelt-skin as a cover . . . not for a second did she let Thorkild out of her sight. Her eyes sparkling with joy and love.

And he drifted and drifted.

In the end, he did not even mark that drift himself. The days and weeks passed. Years vanished and he would not know exactly how many, if asked.

And one fine day, he even got married in Greenland—to Seqineq of course.

Yes, he knew what people in Denmark would say. That her face could be more "regular." Her eyes more "intelligent." Her figure more "refined." But he also saw the grateful joy that shone from those eyes, if he so much as stroked her cheek. The belief and confidence she had in him, as she waited at home for him in their tiny room. The way she would stand in the doorway, watching for his return from the hunt or long expeditions with the sled and the dogs. The almost childlike joy and comfort she radiated when lying down with him under their pelt blankets in the dark winter nights, as another blizzard-storm engulfed their settlement and shook the very walls of their home.

He was happy. And Seqineq was happy. And every other summer during the caribou hunting season, when they moved to their base camp, another brand-new chubby child would be found wriggling in her lap.

He had gradually broken off all the ties he had with Denmark. He would smile to himself whenever he came to recall the excitement and agitation he used to feel when waiting for the once-yearly mail delivery to arrive in the fjord by way of a kayak. Now everything at home seemed alien to him and of no concern whatsoever. Not least because his few friends had forgotten him. Even his own relatives never sent word to him. No letter from his mother either. Except that he did one year receive a short message from some legal pettifogger with news of her death. After that, Denmark was cast from his mind for good.

The truth was that up here beneath the North Pole, he lived a long and joyful life. Among these poor but hardy and discerning people, he came to know the kind of happiness he could never have dreamed of when sitting in his desolate loft room in Copenhagen and seriously contemplated suicide. As his thick mane of hair slowly turned gray, he came to discover not just the delights of a convivial home that had been denied him in his childhood; not just the kind of close friendships he had yearned for in his youth; but also a life mission that was acknowledged and made him loved by those around him. Eventually, he became a father figure to all these children of nature. Their counselor and comforter. And when, in the depths of winter in their small stone-built church, or at the height of the short summer under open skies, he gathered his people around him and—in his own rough way and with modest ability—sought to unveil the mysteries of life and death, he was in fact able to lift those beating hearts inside their peltskin garb. How then, exactly? Because he himself was so full of gratitude that hymns of praise to life and its Creator came naturally to his lips.

It was up here that Thorkild became an old man.

3

WHY THEN did he not—as we know—remain up there in the polar regions? Why did he go back to Denmark in the end?—Yes... why? Did even he know the answer to that?

One particular summer up at the caribou hunt, after many moons had been and gone, the fact he was getting old struck Thorkild forcefully. The winter preceding had been unusually prolonged and severe. Thick snow lay on the rocks until well into the summer, and the blanket of ice was still wedged tight and thick in the fjord when he and his family broke camp and took off to the upland hunting grounds. He had already been suffering bouts of some sort of ailment, and these did not lessen when the summer heat finally arrived. Rather, he began to suffer from a slight shortness of breath, which often forced him to stay at home at the tents, pottering aimlessly about among the women and children, rather than being in the thick of the hunt with its raucous shouts and echo of rifle shots.

He was not a man for that. He became more irritable and truculent. And one day, when Seqineq emerged from the entrance to their tent, she found him sitting on a rock, unaware of her and deep in thought with his hand under his cheek. She approached him quietly, and when she placed her hand on his shoulder with the lightest of touches, a shudder went through him. Thorkild looked up at her, but in the manner of one distracted. And when she asked him why he had been sitting there for so long on his own, he simply got up and gave evasive answers.

These "incidents" became more frequent, as did Seqineq's distress. And when he then entered their tent and saw her worried face and demeanor, he would pat her gently on the shoulder and smile. But he evaded her searching eyes.

In the end, his closest friends noticed with great sadness that something was wrong with him. They asked him if he was sick. And he would reply "Quite possibly!"

But a much deeper truth was at work. For he was struck by longing... as one seized by demons who, in a dream, hears the incessant bells of his home-ground ringing.

There were times when he—sitting alone and full of ponderings—allowed his gaze to traverse the sky-high barren mountain peaks, over which his once sprightly feet would never race again. And at such times a great longing would come upon him. A desire to once more stand in the shade of the large verdant forests of his fatherland. To stretch his limbs in a lush meadow in full clover. To hear the soft rustle of a rolling cornfield... or, say, to be lying on his back atop a green hillock with his hand under his head, gazing into the balmy air. Feeling the sun-warmed earth beneath him, and the breeze caressing his hair. To look out over marshlands. To see village ponds and to catch sight of the red-legged storks—bringers of good tidings and joy. The speckled cattle in the fields outside villages with their thatched roofs and dust-white lanes of summer. The women knitting outside their cottages, or displaying all their innate grace as they walked with wooden milk pails on their heads. And as summer turned to autumn, the men returning home from the fields with flashing scythe blades across their shoulders.

And when he came to think of his mother, his poor, feeble mother... an urge would rise up in him to see her grave and plant a flower there. A sign of a son's love. A quiet plea for forgiveness after all the sorrow and worry he had brought to her little fragile heart from his birth onwards.

And who knew? Perhaps there were still some old friends who might be more than happy to see him again, and to whom he could relate all his tales about his remarkable life and adventures all the way up there in the polar circle... Peter Brammer, Kristoffer Birch, Anton Hansen... and what was it they were all called again?! Imagine their astonishment, if one day he were to walk in the door and say, "Who am I? Why... do you not remember 'the big bear'? Because here he is, men! Standing right before you!"

The following winter, Rebecca—his Seqineq—died unexpectedly. And after this, he could no longer resist his inner longing anymore. With the first summer post, he wrote home to the government minister with his official transfer request, as was the protocol in these things, and the following year he received his state papers authorizing his transfer back to a ministry in Denmark. He was then obliged to announce this news to his "flock." The sight of these pelt-clad people in this settlement on hearing this news—all looking at him with their wise, angular, screwed-up faces, made Thorkild regret anew his decision; something he had already done the moment he received his papers. These people—his people—were losing not only a good friend, but in fact a "father." But there was no turning back. He arranged for his children to remain up there for the time being. They were to follow the next summer, once he had settled into his new Danish home.

Thus it was that, one day in late summer, "the big bear" landed like a terrifying bolt from the great skies among Søby and Sorvad parish's sedate, somnolent congregation.

Legend has it that the bishop almost succumbed to one of his apoplectic seizures the day Thorkild Müller strode into his chambers wearing his greasy jacket and with his giant beard draped like icicles across his broad chest. Things were not helped by the fact that the diminutive, and overly precious bishop was none other than his old schoolmate and childhood friend Kristoffer Birch. The very same old friend who had featured most frequently in Thorkild's thoughts in the last days of his Greenland exile. And, of course, when Thorkild realized who it was, he crashed his mighty palms together and let out a shout of joy:

"Well by my damned hairy breeches, man! Is it you, you old schemer!! You became a bishop!"

Quite how this audience ended has never been reported, but both the bishop and the area dean quickly agreed that the man was completely impossible—further... they immediately set a plan in train that would, one way or another, "manage" the regrettable mistake that had been made and get rid of this wildman before he could provoke the great scandal that he—without a single doubt—would go on to create.

However, rumor runs quicker than strategy, and news of the arrival of the "White Bear" priest raced like lightning across the whole diocese. All around the parishes, word began to spread about the way he would suddenly just appear for the first time in his dogskin skullcap and wielding his long, sturdy staff. How he had frightened children and upset the ladies, some of whom ran into their homes and hid behind their doors. Another tale told of an old man left half-terrorized and stupefied, because Thorkild had suddenly stopped in front of him, planted his heavy hand on the old dodderer's shoulder, and said:

"Here in front of you, my pale friend, you see a veteran bear hunter and explorer of the Arctic wastes, who has seen and experienced things—oh Father mine—that neither you nor anyone else here could even have dreamed of... So be of good cheer, my man! No reason at all to be shaking in your bootees. For fear not. We shall find a way to overcome all ills, you and I. That is written in your honest face!"

There is no doubt that Pastor Müller noticed the strong reaction he provoked from many of those he encountered. But, in his essential innocence, he regarded it as an expression of reverence. A natural respect for a man who had lived such a long and extraordinary life so far from his homeland. In other words, he had put all the torture and travails he had endured in his youth long behind him, and was, after forty years' absence, far too accustomed to praise and respect on account of his personal attributes to grasp the fact that down here in staid, plodding Denmark people might not exactly admire and envy his fortitude and tenacity, his powerful figure and proud beard. Thus, rather than, as in his youth, feeling oppressed by his own "oddness" and incapacity, he cheerfully and confidently walked every parish in exploration. In particular, he paid a visit to all the rectories close to his own abode, in the hope of meeting old theology student acquaintances. And at the most popular Christian and folk revival assemblies, which drew huge crowds, he made himself prominent—not without a certain vanity also, it must be said, his blue and frost-weathered nose notwithstanding—by sitting in the most visible places; thereby making his gaucheness and lack of propriety so obvious that even the schoolteachers present took great offense.

In the end, hardly a day went by without some rumor regarding yet another White Bear "incident" that caused his fellow priests to blush with the shame being brought on their profession and calling. There was, for example, the moment when, at a large country wedding to which he was invited, as the parish priest, Thorkild had suddenly pulled up his leggings—for in no way could they be described as trousers—to his knees, in order to show off his massive calves to the startled guests. Then hadn't he manhandled the bride herself by holding her up, in triumph, to the ceiling with one hand, then looked about him, urging the youths present to see if they could match this feat? At this point, the schoolteacher in the village—a small, wizened family man—finally roused his courage and upbraided Pastor Müller; pointing out that his behavior was inappropriate and simply unacceptable. Rural schoolteachers also acted as parish clerks, so Thorkild was being doubly admonished. But in all his effusive rashness, Thorkild's reply came by way of lifting the man and turning him like a windmill, whereby a quantity of cakes, cigars, sugar lumps, and other delights, which the teacher had pilfered and stuffed in his spacious back pockets, spilled out onto the floor. For once, therefore, the ridicule was not just aimed at this white colossus.

His fellow men of the cloth exchanged a plethora of frantic letters so as to agree on a common approach towards this whirling dervish in their midst. Things came to a head when Thorkild showed his dreaded face at a clerical convention and—uninvited, and after the discussion was ended—took to the podium and proceeded to relate his Greenland adventures. Not only that, he did so with a choice of language and tone that brought the chairman to his feet to declare that he did not "have the floor" and the convention was ended. It was this final straw that led to a serious and unanimous decision to put urgent measures in place to finally bring these outrages to an end.

Their problem was, however, that Pastor Müller's parishioners had gradually come to love him dearly. For, once their initial fright had passed, they saw that, behind his outlandish appearance and startling way of being in the world, here was a man who understood them in a way that they were not usually understood by their priests—a man who was clearly no stranger to any of the problems and feelings they themselves experienced, and to whom they could therefore turn with their own travails—be they petty worries or great sorrows. As if here were one of their own. Any dwelling or room he entered, he did so as a man no better or worse than them. Sit at their rough tables and feed his hunger from their plain fare. Drink a schnapps with them without embarrassment. Happily make up the numbers and muck in, without one eye on a chance to preach or sermonize. And with the sick and those on the threshold of death, he did not fill them with Bible language and pompous speechifying, but did sit quietly at the edge of the bed. Spoke plainly and soothingly to them. Yes, he might read a passage from the New Testament to them, or recite some psalm verses, but overall looked to ease their pain. Give them comfort and reassurance.

"None of ye must tremble or lose hope," he would say. "For who of ye has truly sinned? And if ye have, then I have no doubt it is regretted now and there is a wish to make amends. And Our Lord, let me tell ye, is not some kind of surly boots who sits up there with His abacus precisely counting out each fault and sin. For ye shall see my good people that He is kindly—above all—and will welcome ye with open arms into His kingdom."

Not even Thorkild Müller's bitterest enemies could deny there was a stir—new life and movement—in the hitherto moribund mass that made up the Søby parish congregation. A parish flock, furthermore, that had become notorious among ministry-seeking priests because of its scant attention to anything beyond its own temporal welfare. In fact, these people had always believed that the best way to safeguard the cause of their salvation was by paying the priest his annual tithe at exactly the appointed hour and with exactly what was required and no more. They did of course give small offerings during the three great feast periods of the year, as was only right and proper. Yes, it was these very people who were now flocking in ever greater numbers to Sunday services when Pastor Müller was to officiate. Even churches that had been closed on Sundays due to lack of attendance were now opening once more. And when Thorkild Müller went up to the pulpit, his beard flowing down the never quite correctly presented Lutheran frock vestment and associated circular white ruff collar, and without further ceremony threw out a "Good day to you all, my dear friends! Great we are gathered here again! . . . By the way, what hour of the day is it? Do any of you wear a timepiece? . . . Half past ten! . . . Right then! What was it I was going to say . . . oh yes . . . the story of the time Jesus saw this poor widow lady putting her few pennies into the temple coffers . . . this is the story where Jesus shows that a few pennies a poor person can spare are worth far more than what the rich can give. Whose gospel was this now?—Ah, doesn't matter . . . But hold on, my people!—Let me look it up in the Good Book. For it can be good sport to feed the mind and soul with such knowledge . . . Wait now . . . ah yes, it was Luke . . ." Well, this homespun language and convivial presentation brought animation and interest, even to these well-fed faces. Their ears pricked up and not a sentence was lost to them. Sometimes, in the course of his sermon, Pastor Müller could be so amusing that peals of laughter would erupt across the church pews. However, at other times, and especially during the long prayers and exhortations with which he regularly ended his short, pithy sermons, their priest could be seized by such passion and emotion that his congregation was also thus captivated and lifted to that oft-craved higher sphere. So much so that handkerchiefs would be produced on both the men's and the women's side of the church.

In time, as the good news of Pastor Müller's services grew and spread, people from other parishes began attending the churches where he was to officiate. They too had taken a liking to this type of worship. And it was at this point that the resentment of his fellow ministers boiled over. Even a neighboring priest who had previously spoken in his defense did a quick about-turn. This was a priest of the "folk-centered" persuasion inspired by the famous pastor N. F. S.

Grundtvig. A priest, therefore, who liked to make a show of having the common touch. Nevertheless, he too now began to realize what a dangerous creature they were dealing with, and how necessary it was for the reputation of their collective ministry to have this maverick removed.

It was precisely at this point in our tale, dear reader, that a certain would-be reverend by the name of N. P. Ruggaard became attached to the parish.

His sudden appearance was due to an official order that was sent to Pastor Müller from the bishop himself, who though small in stature was all-powerful in jurisdiction. The agreeable tones in which this missive was couched were not entirely unconnected with the good bishop's need to avoid any outward display of harshness against an old schoolfriend who knew a great deal about his exploits as a youth. So it was that Ruggaard's appointment as parish deacon was explained as a kindly gesture towards an aging cleric: "Due to the unusually large geographical extent of the parish and the advanced age of Hr. Pastor." Of course, the bishop's ulterior thinking was far more concerned with the particular qualities possessed by Hr. Ruggaard and a mantra that came readily to his quiet, politicking mind: Fight fire with fire!

Thorkild Müller chewed and chewed at this long, formal letter with its many careful circumlocutions and obscure phrasing. He had, for some time, been very well aware that the embarrassment felt by his colleagues on his behalf was not solely based on awe and envy of his huge physique. Once this had sunk in, memories from his youth came flooding back and the scales fell from his eyes. Now—on reading and rereading the bishop's official order—he finally understood the whole state of affairs.

"Well ye can eat last year's blubber!" he roared, invoking an old Inuit curse, as he smashed his hand down on the table. "They are trying to get downwind of me to move in for the kill!"

But when this "headhunter" finally arrived, and Thorkild saw the small, pasty-faced, and bespectacled individual who crawled out of his galoshes and greatcoat and presented himself as his deacon, his anger collapsed forthwith—he burst out laughing. To Thorkild, sending such a stump of a man to bring him down was so comical that he just had to go into town to tell his friends all about his "lethal" adversary.

However, quite unperturbed as he was by this reception, the new man set about installing himself in his upstairs rooms and unpacking the full wagonload of chests and suitcases he had brought with him. Choosing to work alone, he hung new floral curtains at the windows and placed his twenty-three well-maintained tobacco pipes in a double row on the wall. He then placed a plaster statue of Christ on the wall near his desk. Above his bed he affixed a luminous cross with a divine inscription. However, he was less demonstrative with his substantial supply of tobacco (two whole canisters of a loose blend and three boxes of the cheapest cigars), which he hid away in a corner of the room. The most care of all he devoted to the erection of his "library," which consisted of a collection of old and worthless books he had purchased by weight rather than value from a book hawker, simply to fill up his shelves. And once he had placed each individual book, making sure they were not packed too tight on the shelves, they did in fact cover almost an entire wall. Just as in his Lord the Bishop's own study.

Overall, Deacon Ruggaard ensured that he wanted for nothing in his new place of abode. Right down to the finest detail. He had bought a fine green shade for his study lamp. An ornate ring holder for tightly rolled papers to light his pipe. A roll of candlewick. A brand-new rod of wax for sealing letters and documents. Yes, even a new spittoon. Nor had he forgotten to bring with him his special table coaster to go beneath his water carafe.

When everything was finally in place to his satisfaction, he wrapped his gray housecoat around him, like a bat folding its wings, sat in his armchair—placed centrally in the room—and, with a smile of contentment, allowed his gaze to slowly turn around the whole scene; a smile that revealed his pleasure at being on the brink of realizing a long-cherished dream. The end of a long and arduous journey, whose wonderful conclusion he would previously barely have dared hope for.

The appellation "Ruggaard" had in fact no connection with Deacon Ruggaard's real name whatsoever. The truth was rather that he bore the common or garden Danish surname of "Hansen." His full name being Niels Peder Hansen, to be precise. Though he *was* the son of a wealthy farmer from the lush and fertile area of Jutland down its east coast, where the children are born with a silver shilling in their hand, as it is put in local parlance. At the age of fifteen, he was placed in the grammar school located in the nearest market town, and it was here he executed the first change to his title. It had not escaped his attention that the more refined types in society often had a placename as part of their moniker, and as the Danish word *rug* means "rye"—a highly esteemed grain!—and there was in his own bailiwick a Ruggaard, or Ryestead, as he—with antique pretension—imagined his new name, he was happy to adopt this title—thereby becoming Ruggaard-Hansen. But then Ruggaard-Hansen quickly became Hansen-Ruggaard, so as to accentuate the Ryestead. The obvious next step was to excise the annoying Hansen altogether, and thus it was that he became a Ryestead—a Ruggaard—in perpetuity.

A similar transformation took place with regard to his countenance and deportment. The stocky, ruddy-faced rustic lad of his early youth had gradually been replaced by a blanched owl-face and a plump manifestation. His large round head had sunk deeper and deeper into his shoulders, and his dull eyes now bulged in a short-sighted, peering gaze. As he sat there wrapped in his gray housecoat, his short straw-white hair somehow luminous above the thick, round glasses perched on a flat nose set in completely waxen skin, he looked for all the world like an outsize maggot. One of those lucent yet light-shy worm creatures that emerge, seemingly from nowhere, wherever rottenness rears its head. The very creature that stares at us when we look at it under a microscope—with its large, vapid but covetous and corneous eyes.

Despite the fact that there had been nothing in the way of specific instructions from his religious superiors, Deacon Ruggaard had a perfectly clear and correct sense of what his immediate task in the parish actually was, and then what was expected of him in the longer term. More than anything, he latched on to the feeling that here, opening up before him, was an excellent opportunity to gain the favor of his superordinates—in addition, of course, to being of service to Denmark's Holy Lutheran Church and its reputation. He had, however, been canny enough in the beginning to proceed with the greatest caution vis-à-vis a local populace that had already been led so far astray and made so blind to correct church dogma. Thus, he began his undertaking by quietly insinuating himself among the most influential people in the area and describing himself as Pastor Müller's unworthy subordinate and sincere friend. Only little by little did he attempt—though always only with single individuals *in camera* and with the most judicious language—to spread doubts about Pastor's sanity.

"Ah yes—our poor, dear Pastor Müller!" he might proffer in mournful tones, and still in that broad East Jutland idiom of which he could not be rid, and therefore an abiding reminder of his rustic antecedents. "If only he would grant himself a modicum of rest. Some peace of mind in his old age. For despite his many excellent qualities—and nobody admires those qualities more than I, his deacon—it can hardly be denied any longer that there are clear signs of a most regrettable erosion of his mental faculties. Ah deary me . . . Well, we are all in God's loving hands! Let us all hope it's just a temporary condition!"

But despite all his innate country cunning, the deacon achieved absolutely nothing by these machinations. In fact, so popular was the movement of the Spirit that Thorkild Müller had engendered among his flock that it proved to be the very opposite of a deterrent, and the more that official alarm and displeasure with him were made known, the more they gathered around him as a greater point of pride! Deacon Ruggaard's fury, meanwhile, grew apace. He had envisioned a swift and easily won victory over this Greenland ignoramus who barely knew his Father and Son from his Holy Ghost! But the farmers of the parish gave him a deaf ear whenever he tried to slip his university erudition into conversation. Nor were they impressed in the least by his library of books. Worse . . . it became clear that many of them had been infected by the bad—not to say impudent—

example set by Thorkild Müller—using him in an almost arrogant way and having sport at his expense. They often called him just "Hansen" by way of a tease. And yes... on one occasion, in the presence of Pastor Müller, a young upstart had shouted at him—in public, do ye mind—when he appeared:

"Well here comes Hr. Deacon Ryebread!"

Needless to say, this crass joke amused the assembled crowd immensely. And, of course, Müller himself shot a volley of laughter up to the ceiling, and would at any subsequent opportunity—with great relish and faux ceremony—introduce him to others as:

"My superior—His Excellency, the Right Reverend Hansen-Ryebread!"

But the hour of revenge was at hand for Ruggaard. For on that same howling winter night with which we began our tale, when Pastor Müller—defying blizzard and winter storm, and only accompanied by his loyal dogs—set off into the harsh, freezing night so as to arrive in time to comfort a dying old man, he tipped the final drop into the cup of indignation that caused it to spill over.

The plain, simple old man, who was at death's door, had not by any means lived a pious life. Among other things, he had never set foot in his local church because—as he had often said when asked—"I don't have the right clothes for that kind of congregating." Nevertheless, he had sent word for the priest to get some idea of what was ahead of him on the other side. Pastor Müller duly sat down beside his bed and proceeded to tell him what he believed the Bible had to say thereof.

When the priest was finished, the man lay quiet, pondering. He then said:

"Aye... but is there no eating and drinking to be got up there for us?"

Pastor Müller had to confirm that there was not.

"And neither a wife nor a sweetheart to be got, ye say?"

No—there was no matchmaking up there.

"Does a body not get so much as a chew of plug tobacco either?"

And when Pastor Müller again had to answer in the negative, the old dry beard turned his head to the wall. As if to say that kind of heaven was not a place he cared to enter.

The priest watched the man's reaction and understood its implications. He therefore pondered this for a while. And after a period of gazing at the floor he raised his white head, resolved to speak. All that he had said before, Pastor Müller told the man, was actually nonsense. Because, as everybody knew... in heaven you got exactly what you wanted. And in order to describe this concept he used precisely the kind of language the old man would understand. Thus, he explained that up there in heaven, a man had only to express a wish and it was granted... so if he were hungry up there, the angels would no doubt immediately set a table for him with the best victuals he would wish. And if he should desire for a wife, he would not be disappointed either—and yes, if he really did get the urge for some chewing tobacco up there, the good Lord himself would hand him a goodly plug. And with pleasure. For He could never deny His dear children, who had died with true faith in Him as their own good Father in heaven. For God just wanted every soul to feel at home with Him.

After this homily, the old man turned his head, happy and reassured. He then folded his wrinkled hands and received the Holy Sacraments, and not long afterwards went to his final rest in the faith of his fathers.

But when this story became known in the parish, a cry of outrage arose from all the surrounding rectories and abodes of parish clerks. To portray Our Lord as some sort of common taproom host and the Kingdom of Souls as nothing more than a putrid alehouse—this was beyond all bounds! The area dean immediately sat himself down to inform—in all confidence—the bishop of this scandal. He concluded with the remarks that there could only be one explanation—which (as was added in brackets) was now common and widespread knowledge both inside and outside the parish—that Pastor Müller's spiritual capacities were no longer without major fault. And further, that it must be presumed he was already mentally disturbed to a very severe degree.

On receipt of this missive, the bishop rapped his hand on his polished desk and made a decision he had been anticipating for quite some time. For via the good offices of his area dean, he announced his imminent arrival in the parish of Søby and Sorvad.

4

LONG BEFORE the peal of bells began, calling the congregation to worship, the little church was packed with people. Every pew, every seat—right up to the chancel and the two rows of ornate cane chairs, and then the high-backed wicker chair in the chancel reserved for the bishop and his entourage—were occupied by grave-faced, yet ceremoniously dressed parishioners. All were gripped by apprehension and anticipation as to what this day would bring. Some were so agitated they simply sat, hunched and bent. Staring down at the folded hands in their laps, as if silently examining their consciences. All the local people assembled there marked well that Thorkild Müller's closest friends had chosen not to attend that day.

Nobody could be in any doubt that this episcopal visitation was extraordinary. All the parishioners being aware that a bishop would only grace the parish with his presence once every several years. Moreover, the whole scene was staged by the church authorities to make clear to the populace that this was a process meant to intimidate and chastise them. And to that end, just prior to this ceremony, Deacon Ruggaard and the parish schoolteachers had been diligent in making clear—by way of quiet word and sign, of their solemn and grave faces—that something momentous was imminent. Word was also spread that, during this extraordinary occasion, not only were all the parish schools to be thoroughly inspected, the church buildings, the cemetery, and all conditions generally would also be investigated. His Excellency the bishop had also demanded that—at this specially convened church service—the parish confirmands from the preceding five years should be called forth for a personal audience with him on the floor of the church.

However, in the intervening time, Thorkild Müller had not rested on his laurels either. The purpose of these arraignments was only too apparent to him, as he made clear to his friends about the parish: "Well, if they want war, then war they will get!" Indeed, for quite some time now—pricked by the constant machinations and sly attacks from his neighboring priests—he had felt the urge to rear up on his hind legs, just as a great bear would do when pursued by howling dogs. Gain instant respect by grabbing one of the sniveling curs by the ears and shaking it senseless. On his long, solitary walks across the rolling landscape, all bedecked in the shades of fertile green spring—the very gentle, slumbering countryside, wreathed in morning mist, that to him was a metaphor for the diffuse miasma existence of his own soporific youth—he had even tumbled his mind with bold plans to incite a general campaign among the people. A crusade that would break the tyranny of false reverence once and for all. He would sometimes be so seized by his urge to fight back that he would positively snort with rage. His visions swarming with tiny arrogant priest figures, who shouted at him and gesticulated their aggression and threats. And as he watched, in his mind's eye, that whole black-clad, pipe-collared gang trooping up, in rank after rank, with those soft-bellied bishops bringing up the rear, the same wild glint would appear in his eyes, the same fire in his cheeks as in the old days of the furious caribou hunts on the great plateaus beneath the vast ice sheet in the far beyond.

The announcement of the bishop's "visitation" was viewed by Thorkild, and by everybody else, as a deliberate signal that he was to be removed as parish priest. And this did away with any lingering caution in his mind. Without being particularly clear about his final goal, his urge now was to preach rebellion. To plant revolution's banner deep in the hearts of the Danish Lutheran faithful, "Those fine reverences and bishoprics will now truly realize that they have let a White Bear loose in their sheep pen!" he would tell his people as he roamed about the parish.

Without sensing the unease that rumors of the bishop's coming had instantly aroused among his formerly so loyal congregation, Thorkild's response to the gauntlet thrown down by his fellow church officers was to plunge ahead with a series of personally conceived initiatives that were of far-reaching significance. Among other things, at the most recent parish council meeting, he had announced that all tithes for the upkeep of his office, as well as offertory contributions, ad hoc payments, and the like, would henceforth be abolished. His argument being that the free use of the rectory and its adjoining lands and property was ample payment for the work a priest performed, and that this lifelong taxation, along with other fees demanded from the population by dint of weddings, baptisms, and confirmations, tended to corrupt the relationship between the priest and his congregation.

But it was precisely the extraordinary unselfishness Thorkild demonstrated in these troubled days that proved to be the fatal flaw in his stratagems against Deacon Ruggaard's suddenly growing influence within the congregation. The suspicions regarding Thorkild's sanity, which this servant of the Lord had hitherto in vain sought to infuse into the minds of the people, now found rich nourishment among these hardheaded farmers. That a priest would not accept offertory takings and their tithes—monies to which he had every legal right—everybody could now see that these were the thoughts of a maniac!

Thus, there was a general, unobtrusive backing away from Thorkild after this day; and when he finally realized that his former friends were beginning to desert him, he then sought to engage with them with increased vehemence, a heftiness that only made matters worse. In one fell moment, it had become clear to all that here indeed was an insane priest with whom they were dealing.

In the preceding two weeks Pastor Müller had raged around the villages of the parish like a wild beast; his intent being—one moment by blunt threats, the next by persuasion—to resurrect his fallen reputation. But wherever he went, he found the farm gates to be either firmly closed, or that the men had slipped away to hide in the stables to avoid having to speak with him. This meant the wives had to receive him in their sitting rooms and humor him until he went on his way.

In some places the dogs had even been set on him from pure fright, after he arrived at the gate or door with his huge oaken staff, frantic hair, and that white beard fulminating from his gaunt face so twisted in anger. His clothes, also, were the road-bespattered, filthy robes of a wandering wayfarer. After those visits where he had actually gained entrance, all handles and locks were thoroughly cleaned—for it was common knowledge that the sweat from a lunatic's hand gave a body the liver sickness!

He had even invited his friends to a meeting at the "hovel" to marshal his forces on the night before his public impeachment. Nobody came.

Such were the background events, as the congregation assembled with bated breath on this day. Their minds astir with all the possible outcomes they could envisage. Here was the explanation for their stooped and downcast demeanor, where they sat with their hands folded in their laps and staring at the floor. As if by these gestures they gave public signal of their remorse, and renunciation of any association with the man over whom judgment was now to be passed.

The priests of the diocese began to take their seats. With their long black garb and medieval snow-white ruff—the so-called pipe collar—so distinctive of the pomp and majesty of the Danish Lutheran state church, they arrayed themselves on the two rows of sturdy cane chairs in the chancel, from which they cast stern glances to the sinful souls below. Those wayward sheep who had strayed so far from the fold. And up in the narrow, sacred space behind the altar, Deacon Ruggaard paced back and forth with his hands behind his back, muttering loudly to himself, so great was his animation. He positively glowed with triumph and anticipation. Now could he truly envision his clerical prospects through the prism of a profound and radiant perspective. The very end of that bright rainbow being the domed chapel of the royal palace in Copenhagen itself, where he—a lowly village boy, the despised and ridiculed "carrot cruncher" student—would stand in front of the altar, all attired in his bishop's regalia, with the much-coveted gold-brocaded chasuble and the Commander's Cross of the Order of the Dannebrog around his neck. Fitting vestments for performing divine service for the royal family, and the most esteemed statesmen who commanded the grave affairs of the nation in the ancient halls of that same palace. And his soul brimmed with gratitude. His eyes with reverent tears.

Outside the church gate, some of the parish schoolteachers—dressed in their formal black gowns and white ties—were standing in line, ready to give signal to the bell-ringer up in the tower and send a messenger in to the priests, as soon as the area dean's opulent landau carriage—in which the bishop was conveyed—crested the brow of the nearby hills. The bishop had announced his arrival for ten o'clock—no earlier, no later. At which point, the service was to begin. Later in the day, he would tour the schools and then return to his official residence with the area dean before evening.

But Pastor Thorkild Müller had still not appeared.

"Of course he hasn't!" said the same little, wizened schoolteacher whom Thorkild had twirled like a windmill at the country wedding, and who forever afterwards prosecuted a campaign of vitriol against him with a teeth-gnashing hatred. "Yes of course . . . make the bishop wait! That's him all over, the . . . the . . . yes, bastard, to put it bluntly! I suppose you have heard, Mortensen, what this scoundrel was going to serve the visiting dignitaries for a rectory dinner, only that His Grace the bishop declined any such, ahem, refreshments? Pea soup and bacon, do you mind! Was there ever such roguery in this land, sir? That, that . . . utter bogman."

His fellow teacher, the wide and rotund Mortensen, grunted in agreement.

"Imagine the cheek of him!" the windmill man continued, reddening to his theme to the point of fury. "Look you now, Mortensen . . . nearly ten o'clock, and no sign of him! Wait till you see, that brute is going to raise a scandal. He will not be happy, that man, unless some riot or other is raised in there! Yes, inside there! In God's House itself! By all accounts he was beside himself with rage at home there in the rectory last night. Strictly between ourselves, the deacon told me he had heard rummaging and rambunctiousness downstairs the whole night. To the point that he was terrorized by it! Believe me, man . . .

he is up to something...oh yes. Sure, he won't just go—Ah, Holy God, Mortensen!...There's the carriage!...Quick, Jakob! Ring! Ring, man! Devil take it!"

The bell began to peal, and with his short, stumpy legs, the bustling teacher-cum-parish clerk rushed into the church. Soon after, all the priests followed him back out to the church gate. What was to be done? Pastor Müller had not yet arrived! It was unheard-of! Word had to be sent to him. This instant!

At the same moment, the landau pulled up in front of the church gate.

Out stepped the bishop. This short, bone-thin man, with a narrow, scrutinizing face. His whole air and regal deportment smacked of authority. He nodded a curt, rather cold, greeting to his assembled priests. Then he looked about him and asked in clear astonishment:

"Is Pastor Müller not with us?"

At this, Deacon Ruggaard sidled out from the cluster of priests—his colorless eyes veritably bulging over his spectacles in humble eagerness to be of service. He announced that Pastor Müller had, unhappily, not yet presented himself, but that a message would be sent to him in all haste.

The bishop eyed Ruggaard with a cold expression that could never have been interpreted as affection.

"Deacon Ruggaard shall do no such thing. Pastor Müller knows very well that the service has been arranged for ten o'clock. It is still a minute short of that...We shall enter forthwith."

In the same turn, the bishop's gimlet eye caught sight of the round shape that was schoolteacher Mortensen, who paraded at the entrance—all pale and puffed from having to stand upright for so long.

After fixing his gaze on him for some moments, the bishop rasped a question:

"What is your name, Hr. Parish Clerk?"

So flustered was Mortensen that his name got stuck in his throat, with the effect that the other parish clerk—the same windmill teacher—in deep reverence and with his top hat held firmly against his chest by his two hands, finally found himself obliged to answer for him.

The bishop then switched his penetrating gaze to windmill and addressed him in even harsher tones:

"That man, I'm sure can speak for himself. And what is your name then, Hr. Parish Clerk?"

"Mikkelsen!"

"Ah, yes . . . of course," said the bishop—the distaste in his emphasis unmistakable—as he proceeded into the church, followed by his pipe-necked train of priests.

Mikkelsen and Mortensen looked at each other in mutual wonder and then with astonishment at the world around them.

"What did he mean by that?"

"Well . . . God knows."

"What was it again he said?"

"Did he actually say anything at all?"

"Nay . . . I heard nothing."

"Passing strange all the same."

A mighty stir rippled among the church's packed pews as the bishop stepped into the chancel. He was small of stature, but most severe of deportment, and wearing his silken gown with the shimmering Commander's Cross as its breastplate. After casting a swift adjudicatory gaze out across the congregation, he sat down in the ornate, high-backed wicker chair. His priests then duly took their places in the rows of cane chairs behind him, and for a moment there was such a profound silence in the church that the only sound whatsoever was the plaintive bell in the tower.

Then that, too, fell silent.

Mikkelsen, the parish clerk, stuck his head out from his cubicle and looked for guidance from Deacon Ruggaard, who then gave the area dean a questioning look. He then looked directly at the bishop. But the Reverend Bishop remained still and inscrutable, with his hands folded in his silken lap and looking straight ahead.

Only at this point did this parish flock down in the body of the church realize that Pastor Müller had not come to the service, and that *he* was the cause of the waiting.

A general unspoken consternation now ensued. Was he really going to make a fool of the very bishop himself? Now that, by God, really was beyond a joke! . . . Everyone's eyes turned once again towards the bishop. All over the church, folk craned their necks and stood on tiptoes to get at least a glimpse of the ever-darker, pursed expression on his wedge-thin face.

Finally, the bishop slipped his hand inside his vestment robe, pulled out a gold watch, and then gave a nod to Deacon Ruggaard, who was standing like a febrile cat beside the altar. The deacon gave the nod to the parish clerk, who then stepped forward to call the people to prayer in the name of the Father, the Son, and the Holy Ghost, and begin the service.

All bowed their heads. The opening prayer was said and the singing of the first hymn began. But for every verse sung, the tension among the congregation increased tenfold. For Pastor Müller was still not to be seen at all, and his place at the altar as the intended celebrant was still empty. Worse, many parishioners could see that Deacon Ruggaard was—via the area dean as intermediary—conducting negotiations in this regard. But the bishop was seen to shake his head, with the effect that the priests were turning to each other with questioning looks.

Once the hymn was over, a further wait ensued, during which the whole church was again so quiet that an audible groan went through the congregation when a man down in one of the back seats dropped a heavy hymnal on the polished floor.

All at once, the bishop now rose from his chair and went up to the altar. He then produced his handkerchief and wiped his mouth methodically. After this, he turned to the congregation and began the altar service as part of the divine Mass.

After such tension, the assembled parish folk were moved beyond measure, to the extent that many had tears in their eyes. As the bishop's beautiful, well-trained, and cultured voice, in all its modulations, anointed their heads, they were gripped by the rare, high-ceremony of this occasion. A feeling of close belonging—of safeguarding and peace—that they had not known for a long time visited all of them. It was as if loving angels had once again taken up residence in their house of God and its resounding vaults, from which Pastor Müller had scared them away with his booming, terrifying voice.

When the Mass was over, a new hymn-singing was begun. A hymn with many long verses, but there was hardly a person in the church who was any longer able to follow the words. Rumor had now spread that Pastor Müller had been sent for. But the hymn faded to silence without any sign of him.

Of a sudden, there was a commotion among the priests. The area dean stood up and nodded to the parish clerk, who hurried from the church. Shortly afterwards, it could be heard that the door behind the pulpit had been opened and the back stairs were creaking as they carried steps... At last! He was here!...

But when, instead of Pastor Müller's wildman head, Deacon Ruggaard's maggot-pale face was seen to appear over the ledge of the pulpit, a general understanding quickly spread that something final had happened and a quiet shudder rippled through the congregation.

Only after the final prayer, and the end of the service being declared, did the parish flock finally discover the whole astonishing story as they streamed out of the church: the White Bear had—without warning, or a by-your-leave—left the district in the middle of the night! The only things he had taken with him were his dogs and his oaken staff. And on the rectory door, he had left a farewell greeting written in chalk:

YOU GET THE TYRANTS
YOU DESERVE

Nothing more was ever heard in Søby and Sorvad parish from Thorkild Müller. Eventually, word did arrive that he had traveled back to Greenland by the next available boat.

Perhaps he lives up there to this day.

THE REARGUARD

I

ONE BRIGHT and sunny morning in early December, a tall, powerfully built man was to be seen making his way up the Via del Tritone in Rome's Centro Storico. He wore a thick blue peacoat and his bulldog countenance glowered at anyone he met along his way. But for all that, and in the manner of a man who was bound for some great delight, he hummed cheerfully to himself as his long strides hastened his passage.

This was none other than the controversial, not to say infamous, Danish painter Jørgen Hallager. Or "Red Jørgen," as he was widely known, partly because of his fiery hair and beard. More formally, though, because he was considered the leader of a circle of young radical painters—the so-called Dregs group—which for a decade now had scandalized Danish art lovers and provoked a rising commotion with its revolutionary crusade in the name of social realist art.

When he approached the crest of the rise, he entered Piazza Barberini, where at its center Bernini's massive marble Triton blows his superb silver column of water skyward to the lucent blue vault. Here, he paused for a moment to get his bearings. Then he cut across the square towards Via della Purificazione.

Jørgen Hallager was still "strange" to Rome. He had only arrived there a few days before and the cause of his visit was his marriage to the beautiful Ursula Branth, only child of State Councilor Branth, the well-known connoisseur of the arts and one of the Conservative regime's most favored figures in Denmark. Indeed, the strong rumor was that Hr. Branth had the ready ear of the minister himself, where matters of theater, literature, and the fine arts were concerned.

"Scoundrel!" Hallager muttered as his mind strayed to his father-in-law; his grimace soon replaced, however, by a triumphant smile that spread across his broad lips.

The marriage ceremony had taken place the day before at the ancient Capitoline Hill site itself. The bride's father gave her away, witnessed by the Danish ambassador to Rome and one of Denmark's most esteemed Supreme Court barristers, Senior Counsel Hoskjær. Also in attendance was one of Hallager's close friends, the young painter Thorkild Drehling, who happened to be in Rome at that time. For the wedding celebrations that evening, Ursula Branth's father had invited the whole of Rome's Scandinavian colony to a lavish feast in one of Rome's most exclusive dining locales, which establishment had been tastefully decorated with Nordic flags and heraldry. The restaurant's imposing busts of famous artists were also garlanded with laurel wreaths for the occasion.

Hallager growled at the thought of the torturous fires he had to suffer all that previous day. He regretted his momentary weakness in yielding to Ursula's deliriums and letting his father-in-law get his way. But that would never be repeated! . . . And damn it anyway. He was not going to waste his time worrying about it. The whole charade was over and done with now and he was the happy victor!

Belying his massive frame, this thirty-three-year-old colossus took the steep set of stairs and landings up to his corner apartment with a lithe alacrity. On the way, he hurled an *echt* Danish "*God morgen*, madam" back down the stairs at a rotund lady who had emerged from the ground-floor closet. This was the janitress who now stared in amazement at this strange bridegroom who had left the marital bed and his *bella donna* before cockcrow.

The newlyweds' apartment was a loft suite on the fifth floor. The morning-fresh bridegroom threw his hat onto the coat stand in the hall and stepped into the somewhat low-ceilinged, but very spacious, sitting room. The fragrance from freshly cut flowers pervaded the air, buoyed by the joyous sunlight cascading through the two open balcony windows, which were framed by ornate exterior shutters. An oriental carpet, portières, decorous curtains, and dramatic leaf plants brought a note of charm to the room's otherwise spartan furniture arrangement—this latter quality having been expressly required by the Nordic guests who were likely to stay for some time. Some old copper antiques, Japanese fans, and other decorative efforts sought to give a subtle imprint of an artist's dwelling.

"Is Her Highness up and about?" Jørgen asked in horrendous Italian. He was addressing a twelve-year-old girl, who was the janitress's daughter. She had been taken on as a maid to the bride and groom. He could just about interpret the girl's awestruck reply.

"La signora rang the bell just there now, signore. She is doing her toi-let. I have prepared the breakfast table inside for signore and signora."

"Right . . . very good, er . . . what is it you are called again? I mean . . . what is your name? . . . What do people call you?"

"Ah! Annunciata, signore!"

"Ah yes . . . listen, little Nuncy . . . go out to the kitchen and stay there until we call you. Stand easy. *Comprende?* Go on, off you go. Psst—away with you!"

This stub of a girl grabbed her broom from the floor and slipped, quick as a hunted mouse, from the room. Jørgen approached the bedroom, which adjoined the sitting room, and knocked at the door.

A muffled scream sounded from within, followed by calls of alarm.

"Hallo!—It's only me," he chortled.

"Well you mustn't come in, Jørgen," the pleading voice chimed. "Do you hear, my love?"

"Ursula! No need for theatrics. Anyway, you have locked the damn door, you little daftie."

"Ha, ha . . . but you mustn't wait there. Please depart from the door forthwith, sir!"

"You really are a tease! But all right! I obey! . . . Can you hear me? I'm walking around the sitting room now. Inspecting our digs, dearest. I didn't really get a chance yet. Ye gods! Talk about opulence! And were there ever so many flowers in a room? Ah look . . . the wedding gifts, are they? Have you seen the calling cards attached to them, Ursula? Let's see . . . 'A. P. Hoskjær—Supreme Court Senior Counsel.' Hmph . . .

I humbly return your gratitude, Hr. Advocate! Never in my wildest dreams did I think I'd be graced with Your Travesty's bumptious presence at my wedding. 'Wilhelm Folehave, author.' And the same to you, oyster-face! 'Honorius Krack, sculptor.' Ah, you regret, good sir, that my hammer hand didn't get the chance of shaking your cloven hoof in greeting, do you? Time enough, pudgy-features, time enough! Let's see here, 'Arvid Petersen, genre painter'... Genre painter? Now that's a good one! I swear I nearly spat out my consommé at the sight of his lickspittle mug—Right, Ursula," he cried in impatience, interrupting himself in full flow, and moving again to the bedroom door. "Come out of that damn room, this minute. The tea will be stone-cold."

"Yes, I'm coming now, Jørgen. Just move away... and I'll come out."

"But this whole show is ridiculous!"

"But you have to move away, Jørgen. Have you?... Promise?"

"Yes... yes! For once I am patience itself! Standing well back now, Ursula!... But wait—ah yes, I forgot!" he muttered to himself, thrusting down into the pockets of his peacoat. He had indeed forgotten that during his dawn wanderings he had gone into a *forno* and bought pretzels and pastries as a surprise for his bride. He now moved over to the small round breakfast table beside the plants, swept a bouquet of flowers away, and dumped his half-destroyed booty into the middle of the pristine tablecloth—Annunciata's diligent decoration and table-laying all to naught. The bakery bag itself he crunched into a tight ball and, in the true bachelor spirit that still reigned in him, fired in the general direction of the stove and its surrounding classical mantelpiece.

While he was thus employed, the bedroom door was quietly opened. A young, dark, and finely shaped woman now stood there in a white morning dress. Her delicate hand resting on the door handle. Jørgen strode towards her, his vast arms ready to embrace; at which she—almost defensively—raised her free arm to her face and pressed her whole self up against the doorframe.

Jørgen all but lifted her into his arms.

"Does your husband not even get a kiss!" he said, as he pushed her arms down. "What's this? Have you been crying? . . . Ah no . . . Ursula! That won't do . . . Do you remember what you promised me last night . . . Have you forgotten already?"

"But I am not really crying," she said, suddenly throwing her arms around his neck."I am yours heart, body, and soul, my love."

He took her petite head and all its mass of tresses and brown curls in his big hands and kissed her.

"And you really love our apartment?" she said, stroking his close-cropped red hair with both hands. "And you think you'll settle and be happy here . . . don't you?"

"Well yes . . . of course. It's all bloody marvelous. Too marvelous and swanky, almost. So this is what kept you so busy before I arrived. Your letters kept this quiet. But I had my suspicions."

"But Jørgen . . . you haven't seen the absolute best thing yet. Come!"

She took him by the hand and led him to the shutters beyond the two balcony windows and pushed both of their wings right back. They stepped out onto a wide balcony.

It was as if they now stood atop a high tower. The Eternal City and its seven hills revealed before them—one half shrouded in wreaths of mist, the other half illuminated by bright morning sunshine. Like a single temple boasting thousands of steeples, the great mass of domes and church spires soared upwards into the richly gilded air. And far to the west and south, far beyond the smoldering lowland Campagna, the snow-tinged peaks reared skywards like a celestial chimera against the deep blue sky.

"Well I never, my love . . . this is really not bad at all!" said Jørgen, after a few moments of silent contemplation, during which Ursula had watched the changing expressions on his face with extreme attention. "I must confess, it's a whole panorama! It beats anything . . . anything! . . . Look at that dome over there! It must be Saint Peter's. God or no God, how it pulses and swells! . . . I tell you, this is a very good spot!"

"Yes . . . Yes. Isn't it just, darling!" Ursula cried as she once again—as if released from a great anxiety—threw herself around his neck.

"Can you understand now that I could not bear living among all this beauty without you by my side? Oh Jørgen, Jørgen . . . you cannot fathom how I have missed you so terribly. How unhappy I've been, having to wander about down here knowing that you were trapped up there in all those storms and horrible icy weather. All that grim, flat ugliness at home in Denmark! Unbearable!"

"Easy now, Ursula! Easy! Don't go getting all worked up and overwrought again," said Jørgen, letting his hand glide down over her hair, which from its middle parting was tight against her scalp but rose in thick waves at her forehead. These were then gathered in a knot at the deep nape of her neck. She was so much smaller than him that she had to lift herself on tiptoes to embrace his shoulders and throat. Her whole figure was so fine, so ephemeral in its grace, that the stark contrast with her husband's massive form veered towards the threatening. At this moment, he was reminiscent of a large, half-tame forest troll, who momentarily suffered a nymph to bestow him with caresses.

"So you are no longer vexed, Jørgen? Yes, come on, admit it, you devil man! You weren't exactly overjoyed that I lured you down here. I could sense it in your letters. Am I right? Do tell me, Jørgen. It's fine. I won't be angry, I promise . . . You thought it was one of my flights of fancy, as you always call them. Didn't you? But now you are here. And have seen! You are not vexed anymore? Are you, Jørgen, sweetest sweetheart of all sweethearts . . . hmm?"

"No. Not at all. I have already told you that, my love! But since you mention it, I'll happily admit your sudden talk of a wedding and then the invitation knocked me off my easel. As you know, I had set myself to staying in my garret and slogging through the winter. So I had my hands full with work and commissions and it was no easy task to get free of them . . . especially not right now, let me tell you." He eased himself from her arms and set his jaw to speak further. "Things are really going to hell in a handcart at home. Folk have got so damn lily-livered and pathetic. It's infuriating. Instead of us joining together to build the greatest resistance possible to protect what tatters of freedom we have left, all we hear is excuses and evasions. And of course our hero scribes are at the front of the pack, demanding nothing other than good weather and lashings of lard for their fat bellies. Dogs and slinking curs! . . . You have probably heard that Sahlmann has gone over to the Conservatives. And with a shameless fanfare to boot. He is even writing for that rag *The Daily Recorder* every day now."

"Who? . . . Ah yes . . . Yes, Sahlmann," Ursula said with a distracted air, as she fumbled with his hand.

"Now that's what I call a stroke! A tour de force. The flowery windbag! I'll give him lyrical if I ever meet him . . . But look . . . what do you expect from the likes of him? For all his Byron bombast, he has never been anything but a long strip of a wet dishcloth. A spoiled child. And that's more or less the way they all are in our once proud Denmark. Our great curse! Not a bit of backbone among them. All show and nothing of substance behind it. Spewing frothy lyrics and prancing rhetoric. Spare me!"

"But you've forgotten all about the view, Jørgen," Ursula said, interrupting him. "Look how the Alban Hills are glistening out there! Isn't it just a beautiful sight?"

"Ah yes, it's nice . . . very nice. But look, Ursula . . . we really have to get something into the breadbasket.. I'm as hungry as a wolf."

They went back into the sitting room and sat at the table.

Without further ado, Jørgen split and buttered two rolls and dipped one pastry after another down into his tea. Ursula, on the other hand, barely ate. She now sat quiet. Reclined in her high-backed antique armchair. Resting her hands in the lap of her white, semi-transparent morning dress, which—in the classical style of yore—was draped closely around her body like ancient Greek robes. With a gaze that radiated tenderness and bliss, she looked unceasingly at Jørgen and relished the sight of his manly gusto. Every now and then, as he looked up from his morning *colazione*, she held out her hand to him. She smiling, with an intimate, heartfelt, "Ah, my dear love!"

When her husband had finally finished eating, she rose to call Annunciata. But as she passed the table on the way to the kitchen door, she was caught by Jørgen's strong arm, pulling her onto his lap. There then followed an interlude of deep silence in which full erotic play and its passions unfolded. The nip and tuck of mutual discoveries that render all talk superfluous.

"Oh you great, big barbarian wild man!" said Ursula at last. "How can it be I love you so madly? Do you remember the very first time we saw each other? You terrified me . . . just the look of you with that great savage beard you had back then. And your rough blue blacksmith's shirt . . . do you remember? And yet it was probably love at first sight. Completely caught. Do you not think it strange, Jørgen?"

"I've no idea, my girl."

"Well, I think about it a lot. Because at that time I had heard and read so many horrible things about you, both in my own home and in the newspapers . . . everywhere in fact. And then, you bad man . . . you were not even nice to me when we met that first time. Not a bit! Very haughty and abrupt, and rude you were . . . nothing like the other gentlemen I knew. But that was probably exactly why I took a shine to you. Do you think?"

"May well be, little dove . . . But wait . . . was there something you wanted to discuss with me? Remember yesterday evening? We were sitting right here and you started on it, but then we started talking about something else. What was it you wanted to say?"

"Ah no . . . not today," Ursula said, suddenly anxious and holding her hand to his mouth. "Today we are just going to be two lovers in love and really happy. We are not going to worry about a single other thing in the whole wide world . . . are we not, Jørgen?"

"Well, all that's done is rouse my curiosity, girl. Was it that serious? You'd better tell me quick."

She sat for a while and fingered his watch chain. Then she spoke in a very quiet voice, without looking up at him:

"Can you remember, Jørgen, you once told me that whatever I asked for on our wedding day, you would not refuse?"

"Did I promise that, ha, ha? . . . Well I better keep it then. My word is my bond, as you know. What are you asking of me?"

"I would beg you, Jørgen . . . I mean, I would ask you, please, to be nice to my father from now on."

"To your father? . . . I think you have picked things up wrong, dear love. Me and your father get on like a house on fire! Didn't I shake his hand heartily yesterday evening? I even congratulated him, and with feeling and with the accuracy of a sniper... '*Un merveilleux souper, Monsieur Conseiller d'État,*' I said."

"No, those small, petty things are not what I'm talking about, Jørgen!" Ursula said with a grave voice. "Oh I wish I could explain myself properly, so you could fully grasp what it is. But it's really true, Jørgen—you must believe me when I say this... my father really is very fond of you.—Oh no, stop it... you mustn't laugh like that. I implore you, Jørgen! Yes, it's true that in the beginning, Father was not best taken with you and our... connection... as he should have been. But you have to remember that he is old-school in all things, and that, at that time, all he knew about you was what he saw in the newspapers and heard through all the bad rumors about you and your friends. That does at least explain things and offer him some excuse, surely? Look how I was, as somebody that loved you... When I think about how even I would lie down and cry all night after hearing yet another scandal about you... So it's not so strange, is it... that Father believed all those things too? Really, darling?... And I know for a certain fact that he has completely changed his opinion of you now, and that it's his sincere wish that a... I suppose... father and son-in-law reconciliation can happen. Now don't be hard on him, Jørgen, sweetheart... you don't have to always be so obstinate! When you get to know Father really well, you will see for yourself how good and loving he is. Just think of all the sacrifices he made for me. Ever since I was a child. Ever since mother died, he has not thought of anything but me and what's best for me. I'm sure he would be happy to live as the lowest beggar, as long as I was happy. And then our wedding! Yes, I am sure he would rather I didn't talk about this, but I can't help mentioning that it was Father who helped me with every single thing in this apartment. Every day he let me drag him around the shops and stores... at one end of town this minute and then the other the next... and bear in mind he is really getting on in years now. Isn't he? But he never once complained, no matter how much he was put upon. Jørgen... he just wanted to make sure we got everything we needed. Fretted over it even, and wanted to be sure you would like these things. Was this the color you liked? Would you like this or that material or fabric? If you liked that kind of fabric... yes, in fact... just imagine... before he decided on the menu for yesterday, he checked with me about the food you like best. Was there a particular wine you liked. And all in all was there anything that would really please you. All this is true, Jørgen! It really is."

"Now listen, Ursula! We speak now as man and wife. So let's be open about all this... that your father, after trying all kinds of—not always by-the-book—ways to thwart our liaison... and when he finally has to cede defeat, and due to his own ridiculous and misplaced sense of honor, tries to, after the fact, put a heavenly glow over our, what he would call, 'mis-alliance'... well... I see no reason, may the gods blast me, to collapse in tears of gratitude, offer warm embraces, and fall to my knees. And Ursula, my love... we agreed most vehemently on that during the time when he devised this Grand Italian Tour for you, with all that guff that you needed it for reasons of your delicate health. Not at all... the only reason he came up with it was in the hope that you—in a new, exotic, and enchanting place and with new friends—would change your mind about that devil incarnate Jørgen Hallager and banish me from your thoughts for all eternity! Do you remember the night before your departure, when we said our goodbyes out at Frederiksberg Gardens? When you threw your arms around my neck and promised I would hear of news of your death-leap into some volcano before I'd hear news you had rejected me? That's exactly what you said. Remember?"

"And have I not kept my word, Jørgen?"

"Absolutely! You have been a really brave and steadfast girl, and I will never forget your loyalty. But that's not the issue here. Not the issue at all... Just answer one simple question: What did your father say when you revealed to him that you were going to invite me down here so that we could be married? What was his answer?... Yes. I knew it. You choose silence!... And anyway, I could have told you beforehand exactly what he was going to say. I know my fellow Danes inside out! He begged, nay beseeched you, to think on it a while longer. Went down on his damn knees and implored you—in the end with tears in his eyes—to delay, delay, delay. Think things over. Examine your heart and conscience and so on ad bloody nauseum. A weeklong dirge it was! And when all that did nothing, he took great offense. Adopted the pose of a proud and loving father suddenly destroyed. Reminded you of all the sacrifices he had made for you. The trials he had endured in his life. And in the manner of a pompous bishop even handed down a sermon to you invoking God's inevitable anger and punishment that rains down on disobedient and recalcitrant souls... In fact am I wrong in saying that in his desperation he called your blessed mother out of her grave in Assistens Cemetery at home, so that her spirit could fly all the way from Copenhagen and join his entreaties to you? Well? Am I right?"

Ursula picked at one of her buttons with lame fingers and declined to answer.

"Your silence speaks volumes... No, dear, and I warned you about this often enough... your father is a sly old fox!"

"Oh—Jørgen! You can't say that about Fa—"

"Yes, protest and intercede for him all you like, Ursula! As I have said before... it really is about time you opened your eyes to the class of people you grew up among. The truth must be proclaimed should it burst a thousand eardrums! Arch scoundrels. Mountebanks. Thieves. Infamous hypocrites... who under the pretext of being Guardians of the Law and Society bamboozle the people, all the better to rob them and the fruits of their labors blind and keep them in misery. And a man who glad-hands those knaves and rogues I am supposed to take to my heart, call him 'friend' and 'dear father-in-law.' Wait... I'll kiss his fat chops for good measure."

"But that is not what I meant at all, Jørgen. All those big things. I am talking about something else."

"So what in hell's blazes are you demanding of me?"

"Now, Jørgen. You mustn't get all rough. And I am not demanding anything of you. It would just make your own little Ursula so very glad and happy if you would humor him a bit. That is all! Oh actually, I forgot! He said yesterday he would pay us a visit today, around noon. So if you would just be your normal self with him. Very direct, but fair, like you are with everybody else. And not this sarcastic 'Hr. State Councilor' form of address. Just use 'De' with him, as obviously he is not a child or one of your chums, so you can't use 'du.' Or even use 'sir' or 'Hr. Branth,' because he is after all an older man and we all respect older people. Or whatever you think is polite, but friendly. Oh Jørgen . . . it would make me so happy."

"Well, if that is all you are demanding, I am glad to oblige. At least then I am spared having to use a pettifogging state title. And anyway, it is very true that I have one good reason to acknowledge your father. Because without him, there would be no you . . . and I wouldn't now be married to my own sweet, beautiful woman doll!"

"There you see! So you *will* be good for me, Jørgen. I knew it!" She took his great shaggy head in her petite, delicate hands and gazed into his eyes. Her lengthy, intense look full of a choking gratitude she could not speak. "Ah, you are so very good to do that. If only people knew your great heart and inner goodness, then they wouldn't be so horrible about you. And if they were honest, it's just the fact they don't like your paintings. My sweet man! Ha! It's so strange to think I may now really call you my man and husband. My husband. My husband! Do you hear? I'm so proud of it, I could shout it all over the whole world! My husband! My husband! Doesn't it sound so wonderful? My darling friend! How happy you have made me! How happy I am. How enriched I am with you."

"Easy there now, little Ursula," Jørgen broke in. He was suddenly restive.

"Yes, yes . . . of course, darling—don't worry. I shan't be overwrought. And I promise not to be a ninny anymore. Now we are going to talk about something else entirely!—Jørgen . . . have you considered how we might spend the day? Do you know what I think? Once father has been here—and he won't stay here for long . . . what about heading off into the hills, darling? Somewhere on our very own, in an out-of-the-way place. Just you and I. No one else. What do you say, dear? Would it not just be really splendid and so nice? I was thinking of Frascati?"

"Frascati? Who or what is that?"

"Jørgen, you know what Frascati is, silly! The quaint little village up in the Sabine Hills. Remember? Do you not remember that I wrote to you about it all?"

"Oh aye!—You were up there one day with Drehling, now that I think of it. And some of the other Scandinavians here. Am I right?"

"Exactly... What do you think? Head off there by train... Half an hour or so and we are there. A tour round the village... then up on the slopes a bit, where there are some magnificent villas surrounded by olive groves. About a half mile from the village there are the ruins of a castle with a completely overgrown estate and parklands. And Jørgen, there are statues all knocked over, crumbling old fountains, and then, darling—oh wait till you see it... an incredibly long pitch-dark allée of evergreen oaks, or holly oaks, is it? Very tough and tall they are, anyway, and this long avenue that is unique in the whole world, or so Papa says. That was the day Thorkild Drehling accompanied us. I had just written *that* letter to you a couple of days before about coming down here and jolly well having a wedding! But I had not received your answer on the day of our jaunt, so I was on pins, as you can imagine. I don't think I will ever be as dazed as I was that day. Wandering the Great Outdoors. The lovely sunshine. And everyone was so solicitous and kindly to me. It really moved me. I was so on the verge of tears, I nearly bawled every time somebody broke breath to me... oh I know I know... you would have scolded me, you bad man-thing! And then at one moment, when I happened to be all on my own with Drehling—can you imagine!—well it just sort of burst out of me that I was expecting your arrival any day! I just couldn't keep it in. Oh, I needed so much to speak of it with someone that I was demented entirely. And lo! Your friend and old comrade in arms Thorkild Drehling is suddenly there next to me, and of course he knew about *us* from the very beginning."

"Well well now... tell me quick... how did he react to that? A bit shocked, I doubt?"

"I'll say... You should have seen his face, Jørgen. He stopped stone-dead in the middle of the allée. Two big wide eyes facing me. You would swear he had seen a ghost! 'Jørgen Hallager, coming to

Rome?' he said. 'You now have me at your great advantage, Miss Branth!'...Jørgen...he would simply not believe me."

Jørgen's face reddened visibly. There was a long pause before he could speak.

"I have a bone to pick with that fellow, by the way. He was acting in such a peculiar way with me yesterday at the wedding. I'm worried the heat down here has melted his resolve. Who are these damn French painters he's hanging about with, from what I hear? I don't like the sound of that. The man is like a pair of baggy trousers that collapse as soon as they have to stand on their own. Why the hell is he mooching about down here anyway, tell me?"

At that moment, the doorbell in the hall began to chime.

"It's Papa!" cried Ursula, who ran out to greet him.

Jørgen remained seated. A fleeting shadow flickered across his broad countenance with its short-clipped beard. He bit his lip to the point of blood when he heard Ursula's joyous cry out there in the hall. Only with hesitation did he finally rise and walk slowly across the room. He had just reached the door when his father-in-law entered.

This councilor of state, or "state councilor," as he was usually addressed, duly made his entrance. He was a diminutive, but strikingly handsome man; white-haired and white-bearded, all of which served to emphasize his dark, radiant eyes. A presentation enhanced by his fine sartorial sense, which was literally topped off by the elegant silk hat, which was now in his hand. It was with a muted, but clearly generous, mien that he shook his son-in-law's hand, then turned towards the sitting room and exclaimed with exaggerated gusto:

"Ah...I see that my lord and lady are still at table."

But as though he feared this statement might be construed as stricture, he quickly added:

"Though it is probably I who am too precipitate. I do beg forgiveness, therefore, for a father's impatience."

"We were just sitting talking," Ursula said. "Come and rest yourself now, little Papa dear."

They sat around the still uncleared breakfast table. The two *Herrer* sat down in the two facing high-backed armchairs, while Ursula moved a pouf over to her husband's side, where she sat as close to him as possible and with one elbow resting on his knee.

An immediate silence descended. Hr. Branth—as befits a councilor of state—had been perspicacious enough not to have set aside his hat on entering. He finally began to speak of the unusually beautiful weather—a real rarity at this time of year, he said, and then asked if the blessed newlyweds had made any decision as to the day's entertainments.

"Indeed we have, Papa. We were thinking of heading off up into the hills, by ourselves," Ursula replied, laying particular emphasis on her last words.

"Yes! Of course!" this born diplomat cried, using a bright smile to hide the fact that his daughter's words had demolished a small hope he had retained. "And what is the destination of your excursion, if one may ask?"

"Frascati."

"Ah, Frascati... no better place for two newly fledged lovebirds. Frascati is really charming. A veritable masterpiece of natural and human beauty in harmonious accord."

Though he had mostly addressed his words to Jørgen, his new son-in-law gave no response, choosing to simply sit in a reclining attitude of exaggerated nonchalance, his right hand grasping his goatee beard and staring at the ceiling; as if his father-in-law's words—indeed his very presence—did not concern him in the slightest.

Thus, a renewed and this time most oppressive silence established itself. The state councilor produced his handkerchief, mopped his brow, and then with a visible effort turned himself directly to Jørgen and with a strained voice began an address that had clearly been carefully weighed and practiced beforehand.

"Well now, my dear son-in-law," he said, still striving to preserve a cordial and lighthearted tone, "my reign is now at an end. My only subject... my dear Ursula... has renounced allegiance and fidelity to myself and has chosen you as her future lord and protector. So I suppose I have no other choice than to divest myself of my crown and hand over my scepter into your careful custody."

"That is correct," Jørgen answered sharply and without looking at him.

"I mean to say," the state councilor pushed on, after a short pause so as to gather his composure, "my son-in-law will of course understand the feelings a father has when he releases his child from his charge and places her future and—if I might add—her happiness in another man's hands. The sadness felt at separation is even more natural in this case, because Ursula is my only child. I mean, she is that rare and delicate flower, in which an old man has placed all his hopes for the future, embraced all his joy, and from whose happiness he looks forward to gain the greatest consolation in his old age. I believe I dare say that I always strove—to let her . . . that flower . . . grow and bloom in the light of what for me have been life's highest values. And always free from even the very idea of compulsion, as *that* is a guiding principle for me. Of course, I understand that in many regards, as far as young people today are concerned, I hold beliefs that are nowadays seen as positively Stone Age. And yes, this veteran state councilor holds up his hands and admits that, in some regards, I may well have been plain wrong . . . I mean, ahem, that I, ahh . . . was steeped in certain prejudices."

"Undoubtedly," said Jørgen in the same flat tone as before.

The state councilor broke off again and blanched—Jørgen's staccato words had hit him like axe blows. For a moment he looked across at Jørgen Hallager with stupefaction, then looked at Ursula, who had taken one of Jørgen's hands in hers, which hand she now caressed in her lap. And it was this sight that seemed to snuff a flame in his dark eyes.

Truly, Hr. Branth had made this visit with the genuine intention of bringing about a reconciliation with Jørgen Hallager. For the sake of his daughter's happiness, he would willingly fight down his grief pangs, sacrifice his pride, abandon all idea of his having any kind of venerable status—white hair be damned—and prostrate himself before this man who had beguiled and coerced his poor child into submission. He now understood that all his hopes were in vain. He perceived only too well that a loving father's petition, his tears even, would at most arouse a sneer on the lips of this horrid gargoyle. Like an annoying intruder, an unwelcome guest, he sat here in his own child's sitting room. Just about tolerated. As if it were nothing more than his good fortune that he had not been shown the door forthwith!

The councilor of state abandoned his rehearsed speech and made efforts to resurrect the planned visit to Frascati. Although each word he uttered tormented him like daggers, he launched into an expansive description of a day he had spent at Frascati thirty years before. In attendance were Constantin Hansen, Ernst Meyer, the poet Hauch, and other Danish artists of renown. With a prolixity and awkward chattiness that was entirely foreign to this man of discernment and precision, he waxed lyrical on the weather, the excellence of the *trattorie* they had visited, the expense involved, or rather lack of same, and all manner of other entirely meaningless things.

During this whole show, Ursula sat with downcast eyes and stroked her husband's hand in silence. This was not the first time she had felt embarrassment on her father's behalf when Jørgen was present. But this bewildering babble, whose cause she simply could not fathom, caused her such discomfort that she was on the verge of forgiving Jørgen his failure to change a jot of his behavior towards her father. In the end, and no matter how much she had looked forward to her father's arrival, she now felt nothing other than stark relief when he finally interrupted his rambling and rose to leave.

"Ah well . . . I'm sure I've been sitting here whittling on and therefore wasting precious lovebird time. I should have minded that no one is as fussy about each and every second as two newlyweds," Hr. Branth proffered with a grim smile as he buttoned his coat with trembling fingers. He managed to steady himself enough to perform a ceremonial bow for his son-in-law; but he did not give him his hand this time, and neither did Jørgen's demeanor request such a gesture. Ursula followed her father out into the hall of the apartment. In fact, right out to the inner landing, where she bent over the banister rail and repeatedly called out, "Goodbye little Papa, goodbye, take care," as he slowly descended the stairs.

"Deary me, how Papa has aged in this last while," she said to herself, as she watched his bent shape edge its way downwards from step to step in an oddly quiet, almost tottering, fashion. And inflamed as she was with her own young joys, indescribable pity for him washed over her in this instant; his loneliness, his white hair, his hunched back.

"Bye bye, little Papa," she called down to him one more time. And he lifted his head at last and gave her a long look. A gaze that was redolent of a condemned man's final adieu.

Ursula quit hold of the banister and rushed back to their apartment. With outspread arms she threw herself into her very own Jørgen's giant embrace.

"And now for our day out! Imagine, Jørgen—we can be together the whole day!"

"Aye. And the whole night long as well, my own brave, steadfast lass!"

2

IN THE early afternoon of the next day, a young, intense man was seated on a bench down one of the secluded paths in the Monte Pincio gardens. From here, he had the prospect of Rome to one side and, on the other, a view of the Villa Borghese's landscaped gardens, as well as the softly rounded heights on the right bank of the River Tiber. He was staring out into some indefinite space in the far distance. For more than an hour he had been sitting in this same forward-leaning position, his chin resting on the round ivory top of his ornate walking cane. Neither the occasional sound of carriages rolling past on the road some distance behind him, nor the chirping of the myriad birds tumbling about in the imposing tree canopy above his head, could rouse him from his reveries.

This was Thorkild Drehling, the young painter whom Jørgen and Ursula had discussed the day before. He was the son of a wealthy landowner and had, much against the wishes of his family, devoted his whole being and raison d'être to painting and the arts, even going so far as making common cause with the Dregs group, right from the start of his artistic endeavors. He had, in particular, attached himself to this group's leader, that same Jørgen Hallager, whose daring and challenging social realist paintings had become the object of fanatical admiration and imitation for Drehling. At that time, Hallager had recently exhibited his sensational *A Martyr* painting: a mammoth landscape depicting a drenched and bare plowed field, where a worn-out farmworker lay buried under a collapsed wall at a marl quarry. The man in vain screaming for help from his blood-filled mouth.

Thorkild Drehling was not long in imitating this picture in a pastel depiction, *The Last Samaritan*. There was no real difference between the two works, other than the fact that Drehling's composition depicted a suffering woman who, in the midst of a desolate, merciless landscape, had collapsed under her heavy load of sticks and logs. Additionally, while Jørgen Hallager's picture showed a rather obviously placed elegant carriage with liveried footmen and a similarly clad servant, Drehling opted for an indistinct apparition, which was meant to depict Death bearing a roughhewn coffin under his spectral arm. This latter metaphor, however, earning him a serious rebuke from Hallager, who hated all forms of fantastic or supernatural embellishments.

His undeniable talent as a painter notwithstanding, Drehling's slavish imitations had gradually lent a derisory aspect to this young artist and his work. Rather than the indignation he had fervently sought to provoke, more often than not he attracted nothing but ridicule and knowing smiles from art connoisseurs and gallery-going public alike. But this ritual humiliation, aligned with an increasingly fraught relationship with his family, had simply made this scion of a landowning dynasty even more receptive to Jørgen Hallager's incendiary influence; to the extent that he had simply adopted all of Hallager's opinions on art and politics, and more broadly embraced Hallager with the type of blind submission that this firebrand demanded from his friends and associates. Indeed, exhorted as he was by Hallager to do so, Drehling had finally sent a formal letter of renunciation to his aristocrat father, which was replete with such uncouth utterances and wounding insults that a complete break with his entire lineage and previous circle of acquaintances was effected thereby.

From that moment, the two were as inseparable as a man and his shadow. Whenever and wherever Jørgen Hallager's provocative figure appeared in public, Drehling was to be seen by his side. Though this slim, quiet, and painfully shy heir to landed property did not always go entirely unnoticed—"that lovely painter fella" being one of the epithets for Drehling used by the ladies of the night as they eyed the gentlemen strolling along Copenhagen's fashionable Strøget thoroughfare. Drehling had also been in Hallager's company the previous winter when they met Ursula Branth for the first time at a skating rink. Ice-skating was the only kind of sport to which Jørgen Hallager had ever devoted any significant time; but he had honed this skill to perfection. In fact it might be said that this sport was innate to him. He was the son of a poor schoolteacher from the bleak and impoverished region to the northwest of Ringkøbing in Jutland, where skates often served as a means of travel when Ringkøbing Fjord and its bays and inlets were frozen solid.

It was a mutual acquaintance who had—much against their will, it must be said—introduced them to the twenty-year-old daughter of the well-known state councilor and former head of department—the esteemed Hr. Branth. Young Ursula's affecting, soulful beauty had immediately made an extraordinarily strong impression upon Thorkild Drehling. And during several weeks of freezing weather that ensured frequent skating rendezvous, this fervor grew to a deep-felt passion, which was by no means cooled by the fact that it was clearly not reciprocated by the young lady herself.

Drehling's drastic shyness meant that he could never have opened his heart to Jørgen Hallager about how he felt towards Ursula Branth. True, he did once make an effort to raise affairs of the heart with his mentor, but he soon realized that, on this one point at least, he did not share Hallager's views. Quite the opposite, in fact. Hallager's brusque comments regarding sexual attraction between men and woman caused Drehling great offense with their immodesty. Any notion that his comrade in art might be a love rival would never have entered his head. Hallager's behavior towards the state councilor's daughter was so bereft of any apparent affection that it left him on the verge of protest. More to the point, Drehling knew that Jørgen was "intimate" with a certain broad-shouldered lass in the rumbunctious Saxogade area of Copenhagen, whom he constantly, if brutally, praised as a "gorgeous bit of skirt," and with whom Hallager often talked of "getting hitched." Then came the day that Hallager, after walking up and down the floor in Drehling's rooms, with his hands in the pockets of his peacoat and talking about all manner of other things entirely, finally revealed in the most matter-of-fact fashion—just as he was about to leave and had his hand on the door handle:

"It's true, by the way, if you haven't heard already, that I went and got engaged to Ursula Branth."

If Drehling had kept his feelings for Ursula Branth to himself up to this point, he now confined the subject to the most secret part of his soul. And as if that were not enough, a week later he disappeared from Copenhagen overnight without a single word of leave-taking with any of his friends. Nothing was heard from him for several months and genuine fears grew for his well-being, indeed his life. However, in one of her first letters from Rome, Ursula revealed the surprising news that she had met the very same Thorkild Drehling alive and well at the Villa Farnesina art museum. He had been staring rapt and spellbound at Raphael's fresco *The Triumph of Galatea*.

It had been a sudden impulse that impelled Thorkild southwards to the very fount of life-exuberance and the worship of beauty. And in this way, here in the Eternal City, in his own quiet solitude and contemplation, free of the influence of friends and comrades, achieve clarity about himself and the self-doubt that love's seeds had sown in his anxious and agitated heart and mind. His first thoughts, therefore, after his unexpected encounter with Ursula, had been to pack his suitcase and move quickly on. But Ursula's dark-eyed enchantment and the unconcealed joy she displayed at their reunion; the kindness, yes, intimacy also, that she bestowed upon him more forcefully with each day that passed, as Jørgen Hallager's confidante, as well as the courtesy and consideration with which State Councilor Hr. Branth increasingly and openly honored him; all this had simply swept aside his faltering resolve. Day by day, he had postponed his departure. He had been Ursula and her father's companion on entrancing walks, museum visits, and excursions. And he more than thrilled at even daring to be in her proximity, and was grateful for any little sign she might show him of engagement and empathy. Until that day, when she—up in Frascati, at the Villa Mondragone and its dark, enclosing, evergreen oak allée—had ravaged the enchantment by confiding in him that a conjugal bond occupied her mind and she awaited Jørgen Hallager's coming to Rome at any moment.

That very same day, he swore, firmly and irrevocably, that he would depart... And now here was he taking his final, grief-laden leave of Rome. He sat with half-closed eyes and imbibed the sounds of this profound city, surrendering to his reveries and urge to wallow in his most personal preoccupations, which had bloomed afresh under these Latin skies. A brooding realm he recognized from his adolescence, when he would traverse his father's large forests and yield to the intoxicating soughing in the trees, or when he would sit atop the dunes before the vast sea and his deep thoughts engendered tears and sweeping emotions.

The faint but insistent tones of the noontide Angelus bell from the church of the Santissima Trinità dei Monti above the Piazza di Spagna finally roused him from his trance. He looked at his watch with alarm and rose quickly. Time was running away from him. He had to hurry, if he was to complete all his final farewell visits before late evening.

His first respects would be paid to the newlyweds.

He found Ursula alone. She got up from a small desk by one of the windows and moved to greet him with that discreet, almost shy, aspect with which she received visitors.

"How nice of you to look us up," she said, offering her hand to him. "Jørgen will be back shortly. He just went for a walk to smoke his cigar... But what's this we have heard about you, Hr. Drehling? Papa told us earlier today that you are leaving us. That cannot be true, surely?"

"Unfortunately, Fru Hallager! I've dallied long enough!... Of course, I do so with no great relish, but my good lady will agree I think that I cannot very well return home to Denmark without having seen Pompeii and Napoli. And if I may say so, I would not presume to think that my departure would be much noticed here. For newlyweds, a stranger cannot be far enough away from their door, or so a wise man once said."

"Oh yes... but you, Hr. Drehling, are not quite a stranger to us. You are almost like family. And now that Jørgen is here, we could have had some really lovely times together. I may tell you that my husband will be terribly disappointed if you do in fact leave. He was only talking just now about having a bone to pick with you," she added with an alluring mock-grave smile.

Thorkild's reply was restricted to an apologetic raising of the hands.

"Dear dear, Drehling, if there's no persuading you, we will just have learn to make do and suffer without you. Come and sit down."

They took their seats in the same two high-backed armchairs around the small table by the window where Jørgen and the state councilor had fought their final joust the day before. Thorkild's gaze took in the fine decor and thoughtfully arranged plants, and after a moment's silence he said:

"And I hear Fru Hallager visited Frascati yesterday?"

"Indeed. We had the most delightful time. Warm, sunny weather the whole day. And then a wondrous moon in the evening."

"Well, what more can romantic honeymooners want. And you had dinner at that classic restaurant... in their convivial gazebo in the garden, enjoying chicken livers, I believe, Fru Hallager? And wine from Napoli. A Falernum wine, was it?"

"My my, Drehling. You are well informed!" she cried—a red tinge now coloring her countenance. "One would nearly think you had spied on us, sir."

"By no means, Fru Hallager! I was here in town all day... busy packing and making final visits."

"Well then... from where have you obtained this intelligence?"

"Can you really not guess, ma'am?"

"Oh, wait. Of course! From Senior Counsel Hoskjær." Ursula's dark brow tightened visibly, and she sat in silence for a moment, looking down at the tip of her neat foot. "I know the barrister and his wife were out there. We got the same train home. That is... they were sitting in the compartment directly behind ours, but I would know their voices anywhere. My hearing is so acute, I could even hear most of their conversation."

Thorkild observed Ursula with the utmost attention. Sitting, as she was, with her fine head bent over her hands and the tips of her elbows resting on the upholstered armrests. Still gazing at her foot. During the previous months in which they had kept mutual company, he had become so familiar with the way her quickly changing moods were physically expressed that he knew immediately her mind was now in uproar.

After a while, she lifted her head. It seemed almost to be a gesture of defiance. She then said:

"If I ask you a question, Hr. Drehling, will you give me an honest answer?... I mean completely frank and honest."

"I shall make every effort, certainly."

"Will you tell me...were you, sir...were you very surprised the time you heard that Jørgen and I had become engaged? I do not mean if you were surprised that I revealed it. Did the fact of it surprise you, Hr. Drehling? Was your immediate reaction that it was a strange party?" As she spoke, the tip of her foot tapped the floor in the constant beat of her anxious emotions.

For a moment, Thorkild hesitated in answering.

"So it was this that Hr. Senior Counsel and his wife were discussing yesterday evening in the—?"

"Yes, among many others, it seems! But I am putting the question to you, sir. What was your first reaction?"

"My reaction?" said Thorkild with a strained smile. "Do you really need to ask, Fru Hallager? Of course I found it quite natural. I am sure I have mentioned to you before that from the very first time I saw you... I don't know whether it was something in your bearing and very essence... in your extremely fine sartorial discernment, or in the ardor with which you talked about the free life of the artist. In any event, I immediately gained the impression from you that you had always contemplated becoming the wife of an artist."

"Indeed and I have!"

"And so I find it quite natural, especially since your dear father's home has always been a sanctum—and a famous sanctum at that—for lovers and practitioners of the arts."

"Yes, Drehling... but heavens above... Should I have married ancient H. P. Holst or old Professor Hagen, or that dead animals painter—Karsten something... with the wooden leg?"

"Certainly not, Fru Hallager... not least because these gentlemen are already sufficiently married. But I could imagine—well... cards on the table, since my hostess has shown me that intimacy of inquiring as to my frank opinion—I can well imagine that such good people as... yes, just like the senior counsel and his entourage... that they have difficulty accepting the fact that your choice, ma'am, fell precisely on that man who in every respect stood farthest from your own familiar circle. In fact on that person—of all Danish artists—who has been the least favored in that sanctum of your father's I refer to. If I may put it like that."

Ursula declined to respond immediately. She had leaned against the back of her chair. And as she held her outstretched hands in front of her so that the tips of her slender fingers touched slightly, she looked out of the window with a quiet, yet proud, gaze. Taking in the evening sky and all its redness in the west, the luster of which threw a seemingly revelatory aura about her whole figure.

"Ah yes, I admit it may seem strange," she said finally. She was speaking very slowly and as if she had no thoughts at all about with whom she spoke. More as if she were talking out loud to herself. "But it's just because people do not know the real Jørgen Hallager in any way... that they rush to judgment as they do. It may well be that he is sometimes reckless and just leaps into the fray... but that is simply his nature! Yes, he is obstinate and perhaps arrogant due to the great gifts he possesses... all true! But who else has had to fight his own way through so many obstacles like him? When I think of all the things he has had to endure, right from his earliest childhood—all kinds of humiliations, poverty, and want; yes, even hunger... then I well understand how he got that dark and bitter view of life, for which he is always criticized... But as for the rest," she added after a pregnant pause in which she seemed to offer a prayer with a deep smile to Venus, the evening star, "that doesn't mean he will always be like that."

Thorkild raised his head with a start. His eyes wide in amazement.

"I'm sorry? . . . You actually think, Fru Hallager, that . . ."

"Absolutely," she said, with a slight toss of her mane, her gaze still turned to the evening sky. "Consider your own self, Hr. Drehling! Is it not true that you have become like a new person since you got away from your multitudinous friends and all that horrible, endless strife and bother at home?"

"So if I understand my good lady correctly," Drehling stammered as his countenance reddened, "you believe that Jørgen's change of lifestyle and his presumably lengthy stay here in Italy will . . ."

"Drehling, my dear man, I do believe that the artistic healing power of Rome is close to your heart also," she said, and now fixed him with such a knowing look, he was forced to avert his eyes downwards. "You are so secretive these days, but I have my own ideas regarding your good self, sir—and I doubt I am wrong."

Thorkild did not answer. In fact, he barely heard her last words. A feeling of profound sadness and pity drenched his heart and struck him dumb. Now he understood her completely. She had, with her words, her celestial gaze, her blushing cheeks, removed the last nebula-veil that had occluded her inner life. Her very soul was now exposed before him. In all its proud, romantic exquisiteness. So this was her secret hope! This was the great vision Eros had launched into her heart, giving this young, delicate woman the bulging heart's blood and almost supernatural courage to defy the judgment of the whole world! She dreamed of becoming Jørgen's redemptive angel. His Beatrice. His Laura. Her sacred role!

Just at that moment, heavy footsteps could be in the hallway. Jørgen Hallager strode in.

If Drehling had wavered in the slightest with regard to leaving Rome, any lingering doubt was now dispelled at the sight of Ursula Branth immediately throwing her arms around Jørgen Hallager's neck in obvious rapture and chirruping loudly with questions about his long absence as she did so. He felt all too keenly how the blood fled from his cheeks and the corners of his mouth stiffened.

"I couldn't understand why you were taking so long," Ursula continued, without letting go of Hallager for an instant. "I actually began to worry. Where have you been all this time, you bold thing? Did you meet anyone interesting?... Look what I have for you, darling!"

"Aye, aye, Thorkild!" said Jørgen, shaking his shipmate's hand with full force. "Where have you been skulking, you hammock-louse! I was out looking for you this morning at your atelier, but the front door was bolted. Were you recovering from some mystical starry-eyed night wandering beneath a tragic full moon? Isn't that the latest vogue from Paris with ye tortured artists? Speaking of Paris... did you hear the latest news from there?"

"No... What happened?"

"I was in a café and could see the headline in *Figaro*. Anarchists up there have obviously flexed their muscles. Blew up a swanky restaurant. Some people badly injured and a lady had half her head blown off. Now we have the usual outrage and fury, of course."

"Not again! That is just awful," Ursula exclaimed. She crossed her hands at her chest in the manner of a nun and grew quite pale.

"Ph'rrrr... What else can we expect!" Jørgen cried as he threw himself down on a chair, put both hands behind his head and stared at the ceiling. "There has to be a few eggs cracked to make an omelet, as the saying goes. Of course it's sad with bombs going off and poor innocents getting hurt. But, who knows? Maybe there really is no other way to get listened to in these new times."

"Ah, stop with all that silly talk, Jørgen," Ursula protested. "You don't really mean that."

"Well, no... I probably don't. But at least I can try my best to argue for the true cause. To keep the red flag of rebellion aloft! It's very easy to get flabby and become tainted with bad influences."

At this, Thorkild Drehling rose to leave.

"Eh!? Where the hell are you going, Drehling?" Jørgen cried. Jumping up from his chair.

"As I was explaining to your wife, I am leaving for Napoli this very evening and there are still people to visit."

"Oh no, hold on. Leaving before we get a proper tête-à-tête? And me with two lungs full of curses to blast at you, you blackguard!"

“Ah yes, I forgot,” Drehling said with a rueful smile. “Your good lady Ursula mentioned you had a bone to pick with me.”

“A bone? A whole damned skeleton, my man. And don’t think you can just slip off like this.”

“Well that must wait until my return. As I say, I’m running behind.”

“Right then . . . but be warned, the more you delay, the more red meat will be on that skeleton. Sure there’s not much to be doing down that way, man?”

Without offering a reply, Drehling turned to Ursula and gave a gracious bow of farewell.

Ursula took Jørgen by the arm, and both now followed their guest out into the hall and landing.

When the last farewell had been expressed, and Drehling had reached the next landing below, Jørgen bent over the banister and roared a fiery parting shot:

“And be sure to give Vesuvius my warmest greetings. That old dynamiter! Ask that old giant when he is going to give a serious show of strength so the whole world hears it! Tell him from me that we all need waking up from our daydreams!”

“My word, Jørgen. You are positively raving this day.” Ursula laughed out loud and tugged at his cheek, but her gaiety was, in truth, quite forced. “Whatever will Drehling think of you?”

3

Rome, January 4th

GREETINGS, oh "Clandestine Quill"!

My report to the group is indeed, as you say, overdue. And anyway, it is of course the wont of our exalted Danish *artistes* down here to send home reports of their "Grand Tour" impressions from the Holy Grail of all art itself—Rome. Probably more to the point, it's a rotten rainy day here and as I am, for a change, just in the mood for some quiet occupation at my desk, I have now lifted an implement mostly foreign to me—otherwise called a pen—so as to fulfill your command. Your clearly considerate request to be spared from all lyrical outbursts, of the artistic or Great Outdoors variety, does also help—ditto your request for accurate information on relevant individuals, events, and conditions here, which may be of use to you on the Home Front. Understood, comrade. We are of one mind, old schemer! Have at them . . . thrust and slash to your heart's content!

And by the way (this will not surprise you) you could have spared yourself the warnings about gilding the writerly lily. For my artistic impressions from these nether regions can be well summarized by a marvelous outburst I happened to overhear at the Vatican from a blunt-speaking Swede who was standing in front of a Renaissance sculpture of three stark-naked women. As you might know, these are called the Bacchae by posh people, but our good Swedish cousin was having none of that—"Well, here we have some fine saucy strumpets!" says he. I had the greatest urge to hail that fellow and embrace him heartily. For he displayed a truer and healthier view of art than that whole gang of fey beauty worshippers put together. Ah yes! A blast from the horn of truth can do a man good, even if it does come from a rednecked Swede. Because we are otherwise up to our necks in blind idolatry down here! The other day I got to thinking of what posterity would make of us and those who were here before us. I mean if God decided to extirpate all our creative and created objects, except for those of the so-called fine arts. If, that is, people in the future would only be able to gain an understanding of the past and its people through prancing goddesses, bathing nymphs, coquettish Madonnas, and naked ponces (called discoboluses or some such), and all the other brothel and pederast art, which from time immemorial has been the subject of our hysterical worship. By my red beard, man, I swear... you can walk through a hundred galleries down here without seeing a single reference to ordinary life and the struggles of the common people. Not to mention the human urge for freedom. In fact... nothing. Nothing at all that depicts the constant stir and will to work within the breasts of people—the real dynamic that has kept our world in motion and the driving force of all creation. At best, we might get some shepherd nirvana through a bourgeois perspective, or a scene from a rowdy tavern full of stock characters. Other than that, nursery room fairy tales, heavenly visions, nature bewitchment, and florid laments on unrequited love. Only a few of the very oldest Christian painters, albeit in their stilted depictions of Christ's persecution, have expressed a genuine indignation at the evisceration of truth and justice here on earth, and thereby sanctified artistic creation by deliberately choosing to be provocative, just as in our own time, in which social realist art is finally breaking through.

Now then... I can feel that I'm getting a bit airy-fairy myself here, after all my promises. Enough of pastorals—now for the flesh and bone!

To start with basic facts. From what I am told, this winter there are even more Scandinavians down here in these "Elysian Fields" than ever before. A sign of the rotten times, of course! Here in Rome, this circus consists of around thirty well-tamed animals who jump through their hoops and get fed twice daily at their trough—a thousand pardons—trattoria—which is housed in a set of ancient ruins called the Baths of Diocletian; a disgusting set of ancient hovels, reverently preserved as a holy relic, even though they occupy a huge area right at the heart of the city. An obvious site for a market hall, a citizen's square, or other civic amenity. Now, it is in this stinking rat's nest that a certain Signor Francesco runs a squalid hostelry that is more a dung-filled and filthy cellar vault than anything else. The actual dining area is one of the ancient bathrooms and this has walls three times thicker than a baker's oven. And yes, it is this and its adjoining cellar, with its "painterly aspect," do you mind, that has attracted this pack of Seals, as this rabble, with commendable self-awareness, has dubbed themselves and their fraternity for use at their feeding times. To give this club it its full pretentious title—Ultima Thule Seal Club. Often, they just simply say "Ultima" to each other as an esoteric shorthand and password. Of course, they themselves believe they are following and celebrating the ancient Roman customs of Civitas, Liber Pater, and Liberalia by debating and crushing their mutual grapes so as to toast the arts and carousing in the midst of the populace.

Furthermore, your "Notes from Nowhere" will be interested to know that this year's menagerie consists almost entirely of Danish squawkers, rather than Swedes or Norwegians. A prime example of this is the lion's role that has been awarded to Supreme Court Senior Counsel Hoskjær who, along with his preposterous ape of a wife (at more lip-quivering moments his "heart's boon"), constitutes the core of this insufferable Scandinavian bonhomie. This same lawyer is a three-hundred-and-fifty-pound truffle-fed gormandizer with a corresponding bright and marvelous outlook on life. He constantly admits this himself—and with unsurpassed conceit—that he hates all forms of disruptive dialectics and would rather die than see life's proper order upset in any way. You may note that he is on the tax list with an annual income of half a million or so. And there we have the main reason he cannot get it into his shiny widow's-peak head why there are people out there who complain about life. With his smug, flaming gammon cheeks, he views it as his life's mission to personify the protests against the "reform fever" and alleged morbid negativity of our age. No surprise to you then, and note this well, that in recent times Hoskjær is being championed as "the Man of the Hour" in Denmark, now that a clamor is increasingly being raised from all sides for gifted, noble-minded men of culture who epitomize the effortless cohesion and conviviality demanded by our times. It is already being whispered behind fans and begloved hands down here that his rising star has been noted in the highest of places. Yes. And why not? Perfect! The golden age of the barking seal is upon us! From now on, your social standing will be judged on your wobbling layers of fat! Bravo! Let them eat cake! Only the royal bakers are laughing.

The rest of this troupe consists of the usual motley collection of enthusiastic gentlemen and ladies; dilettantes all, who have come down here to emote about culture and ideals under blue Mediterranean skies. Most prominent, of course, are the fine arts connoisseurs who swan around in these climes by way of manna that falls to them from the heavens—otherwise known as the Ministry of Culture. All in the name of artistic inspiration for future masterpieces! Step forward, therefore: Adonis-Petersen (who, where appearance is concerned at least, has become a veritable po-faced and rapt Raphael—cap 'n' all!); then I give you Ludvig Hegger, and the famous Norwegian sculptor Karl Kristian Honorius Krack. This latter has crushed me—he is convinced—three times at least with his Peer Gynt stare and has openly stated that I defile Rome by my very presence here. The fact that your, ahem, fellow scribe—the poet Folehave—is down here may be known to you already. His tour here is a resounding success, especially with the ladies, partly because, at even the hint of a request, he will present them with a fragrant red-bound copy of his, say, *Ahasuerus*, *Richard the Lionheart*, *Robespierre*, or whatever the titles may be from among the scores of windbag versions he has produced by shamelessly filching from Kofod's *A History of the World*. Truly a plagiarizing "poet-hero," as he is acclaimed back home, who matches these present times. Though it must be said that success has not even taught him to be arrogant! Never in my life have I seen anything less proud and forthright than this sniveling little wretch who seems to have developed a hunchback from a surfeit of bowing and scraping. I swear! The man can barely cross a floor without constantly whimpering, "I do apologize!" "Oh, please don't trouble yourself!" In short, he possesses the requisite stooped neck and cowed civility that has always been even more necessary than talent and backbone to gain admittance to our Danish Parnassus.

Let me see . . . what else do I have to report? Christmas Eve was, of course, celebrated at the Scandinavian Association in time-honored Nordic fashion with *Ris a la mande*, lashings of roast meat, and a jolly swing around a decorative shrub that passed for a Christmas tree. Afterwards there were hymns sung and soft drinks and bowls of punch. Aforesaid Senior Counsel Hoskjær, by the way, stubbed his toe at the end of the night when he missed a step on the stairs. A bit too much Swedish glögg, I think! But I should probably remind you and the comrades that I am not in a position to inform exhaustively on the exploits of our compatriots down here. As you can imagine, I only see them now and again, and when that happens, I am mostly found to be cursing them. But from all of the above, neither you nor our fellow rebels must conclude that I am going around down here kicking over tables and generally acting like a bull in a china shop, despite my fury at the antics of our enemies. Not that I would hesitate, as is well known, but I choose not to do so for a particular reason. Actually, for the sake of a particular person. I believe you get my drift! It is true that I increasingly miss my hard graft, my painter's garret, my world of work, to the point where thunder and sparks fly from me. But, on the other hand, I have discovered that those who claim marriage is an excellent institution are not entirely wrong. It may well be the only thing that is spared when the guillotine is brought into service! This free love idea is all very well, but it's a fop's game and character-sapping. Comrades waste a lot of time and energy chasing about in the streets and night cafés to catch new birds. You may bear this in mind yourself, you old chaser. No more of all those night haunts and vaudeville nights for you, my lad! Truly, home is in more than one sense a man's "castle" . . . I never thought Jørgen Hallager would say that. But never let it be said he will not confront the truth!

I am going to avoid writing anything about the situation back in Denmark. Every time I get news from home, or read the newspapers that are sent to me, my fury boils over. This then makes my present idleness twice as unbearable. But I can assure you that this will—here I emitted a foul curse—very soon come to an end. You will all soon be seeing me again! As soon as possible. But damn it all. Now you have got me started . . . something has to be done about all this backsliding and laziness among our comrades at home, given the corruption we are seeing. Even a half-dead pig will let a squeal out of it, if it is pricked! I have read that Sahlmann has been made a Knight of the Garter in the New Year's Honors List. He has more than deserved it, the cowardly, arrogant cur! Every time I think of him and the other traitors to the cause, I feel like sending them a piece of shit in a registered letter. Express delivery! If they ever get what they truly deserve, they will drown one night in a cesspit and be buried twelve feet down with a latrine barrel for a coffin. The dung company could lay a wreath for the whole lot of them as a grave for unknown shysters.

But I'll stop here. You're probably tired of all this talk anyway. Give warm greetings to Chatterbox and thank him for the letter. And Rasmus as well and all the other steadfast soldiers. If they ask about me, they will—as stated—soon see me back at home. You know that Drehling was holed up here for a while? I didn't get talking to him much before he left a couple of days after my arrival, but he is very shaky-looking to me. I'm worried he's going all starry-eyed and romantic down here. I'll have to give him a good schooling when he gets back to Rome.

Oh wait—one more thing! Behind the clothes press at my digs you'll find (among other things) my painting of a factory girl being dragged off by a cop, while two laughing toffs in tails and pointed shoes watch on. You might remember it? Could you in all haste get a proper frame around it and flog it to some arty banker or merchant type? Or put it in for exhibition with muttonchops at his art gallery on Bredgade in town. From whatever money you get (accept what's offered) send a hundred to the bricklayers' strike fund. Send the rest to me down here.

To the barricades!

Yours in struggle,

Jørgen Hallager

4

THE ROMAN new year came in with muffled exhalations. Throughout the month of January, the Eternal City draped its allurements with a dark veil of fog and rain in the manner of a precocious convent novitiate. The already highly irascible Scandinavian colony was even ambushed by a blizzard one day, just as they were receiving confirmation of a warm and sunny winter back home. It was not until the start of February that the sun began to reappear and eventually unleash its full power and radiance. And as this welcome return coincided with a series of full moons, the Scandinavians decided one lunchtime, at the aforesaid Signor Francesco's, that they should decamp to one of the oft-lauded *artiste-trattorie* in the gardens at Ponte Molle, or to give it its newfangled name, Ponte Milvio. The purpose of this new northern migration being, in appropriate Nordic custom, to welcome spring under open skies and by way of a symposium, which august occasion, of course, would see raised mead- and wineglasses flashing—blessed by brilliant Phoebe's silver-green rays.

Tokens were dispatched to all the other patrons of the Seal Club fraternity, including State Councilor Branth, who seized on any and every pretext to visit his daughter. Branth immediately promised to inform the newlyweds in Via della Purificazione.

The church bells had just rung the four o'clock hour when Branth, his heart racing with anxiety, reached the landing that crowned the innumerable steps that led to his daughter's loft apartment, where (upon his self-declaration as an "*Amico!*") he was allowed in by little Annunciata. His face brightened immediately when a glance at the row of hangers in the hallway informed him that his son-in-law was not at home. With a broad smile, he entered the sitting room. Ursula was sitting in her armchair by the window, busy at embroidery.

State Councilor Branth placed his silk hat on the table and threw his gloves inside the lining. He then walked over to his daughter and kissed her forehead.

"So here we have the housewifely Fru feathering her nest, rather than enjoying the wonderful sunshine out there. Is the man of the house not in situ?"

"No, but he'll be back soon. Sit down and rest yourself, little Papa."

"Hm... I won't, thanks, my angel. I'm in a rush today. I just wanted to call in for a moment," he said, lifting his hat as he did so. "I really must dash. So much to get done today. I presume your husband has gone out to smoke his cigar?"

"No, Papa... he smokes here at home now."

"Really?"

"Yes. I asked him to do that myself."

"Gone for a stroll before supper, then, has he?"

"Not exactly. He went off quite early this morning with his painting case."

The state councilor, who had half turned in readiness to leave, turned around again to face his daughter. A look of astonishment on his face.

"Your husband painting... out in the common street... here in Rome?"

"Yes, why not? It's such a lovely day, Papa."

For a moment, it was as if the little man's face had turned to stone. Choosing, for his daughter's sake, not to think aloud, he turned away from the window to fully face into the room, as if an audience were assembled there awaiting his word. Under his breath, he speculated on his son-in-law's pictorial endeavors... no doubt some mound of pig swill he has sniffed out! A drunken slattern... or the backyard of an abattoir.

"Regardless, my dear," he continued, now in full voice, "I mustn't forget the reason for my visit. The thing is that... our Seal Club has decided to head out to Ponte Molle this evening. There will be a full moon tonight. You might recall I told you about this lovely custom of heading off to that place. It was brought in many years ago... thirty years ago, when I, along with Ernst Meyer, old Hansen, and... ah no, dear... it's too long in the telling. I just wanted to ask if the lovebirds would like to come?"

"Of course, Papa. That would be lovely. Where are we to meet up?"

"We thought Francesco's would be a good rendezvous point, around eight? We'll head off in carriages. How does that suit... you both?"

"I'm sure it's fine. But had you not better wait until Jørgen comes back? We can make proper arrangements then. He'll be here any minute."

"No really, dear, I must go now. I haven't a moment to waste. Goodbye, my little dove." With extreme gentleness, he lifted her chin with his hand and raised her gaze to his. "Are you keeping well... And are you really happy? Your Papa thinks you have looked rather pale lately? In poor form?"

"Weh'... ll... do you think?" she answered with some hesitance. Her face reddening as she did so. "I'm not sure it's that, Papa. Maybe more that awful sirocco wind and rain we had. From the Sahara, you know. Blood rain they call it. Because of the sand. But really... I'm fine. I'm very happy."

"Ah well. May the Lord God watch over you, my child."

With trembling lips, he kissed her once more on the forehead and walked away without a further sound. Ursula followed him out onto the landing, where, as was now her tradition, she bent over the banister to watch and nod to him as he made his way down. She had noticed that he greatly appreciated this gesture. In fact, on the one occasion she forgot to do this, he had been most upset.

"Bye bye, little Papa dear!" she shouted down to him as he stood for a moment at the turn of the last stairs and blew a kiss from his fingers in return.

On her return to the sitting room, she saw he had left his gloves behind on the table.

"Oh Lord, Papa!" she exclaimed. Shaking her head dejectedly. "Yes, Jørgen was right! He really had started to enter his second childhood. The day before yesterday he forgot his walking cane. Before that, his handkerchief. Where was it all going to end?"

With a quick sigh, she settled in her armchair and took up her embroidery once more. However, while continuing to work in a mechanical fashion, she soon sank back into the reveries her father's arrival had interrupted. As the light fell, and she stuck the needle up and down through her canvas mesh, her thronging, ceaseless thoughts flitted first here then there, like a little bird jumping from branch to branch in its nest tree. When she came to think of her father's astonishment at hearing Jørgen had gone out to paint, a smile played on her mouth. Oh yes... oh yes, little Papa! Just wait. You'll soon see... don't worry. All your worries and disquiet for my sake will be shown for what they are... needless. Just a little patience, father!... But if only she knew where Jørgen had got to! Her great hope was that he had gone to the Palatino—the Palatine Hill. Weren't they the ruins of the great emperor? Augustus, was it? Certainly, a profound and overwhelming feeling prevailed there somehow... "As if one were walking among the desolate ruins of a god's workshop," as Thorkild Drehling had once said when he accompanied her there once. This was what her Jørgen craved. Something stupendous. A great and profound idea. Some great, momentous challenge. Only that could move him. Lift him. For he himself was so great and unusual in all things, so vast in all his passions. Ah, you... my great and mighty eagle! How proud and daring your flight will be when you finally lift your wings! How high, high, high you will soar above and beyond all the little wrens and sparrows at home, which prefer the neat little gardens and dirty puddles to wide heavens! As long as you don't entirely forget your little Ursula up there in the rare ether. Keep in mind your very own young mother hen, brooding and clucking here in our nest. Waiting and longing, but unable to follow you!... "And are you really happy?" What a strange thing for Papa to ask! Are there signs of that from me? No wonder with all that rain and fog... everything so sad and gray. She did not blame Jørgen in the least for finally losing patience and looking to go home... that's a man who has to work, if ever there was one. But now the doldrums were over. Now she was happy—really really happy! The great vistas were opening up!

She threw her work to one side and got up. She could sit still no longer; such was her longing and excitement. Surely Jørgen would come soon? The sun had set, for heaven's sake. Here from the balcony window, she gazed at the whole western sky as it blazed before her, like a world on fire. And down below, the city was already half buried by a red evening mist. Oh look! Out there beyond the Campagna, the moon emerging. How lethargic she looked! . . . Not in the mood to shake your feathers, eh? You lazybones! Would you get a move on there. And make sure to shine gossamer and bright for us and our festivities this night!

Then she gave a start. The doorbell ringing? With vexation, she spun around in the direction of the hall. What strangers would call at this hour? She knew it was not her father's way of ringing the bell. Ah . . . just the postman.

At the door to the sitting room, Annunciata handed her a small, neatly tied package.

"Those stupid newspapers!"

She hid the package under some books on the writing desk. Nothing would be allowed to disturb the festive mood. Not today . . . where was it to be held again? To Ponte Molle, her father had said! Yes yes . . . it was going to be wonderful. After such a beautiful and inspiring day as he had enjoyed, and such an evening to come, Jørgen would no doubt really look forward to it. They did not have to be with the others all the time either. They could even walk home once the others got their hackney carriages . . . yes they would walk, arm in arm, along the quiet moonlit pathways. Talking together in subdued but excited voices. Discussing the future and their love for each other. Or maybe they should just stay at home anyway? Hold their own intimate, private love-fest. Here behind firmly shut doors. Sitting together bathed in a shaft of moonlight from the window. Quiet. Not saying much. Together entwined. Mouth to mouth! Should she do that? No no... that would not do. Jørgen would hate all that romancing... Once again she had proved him right. She really had become like an immature girl!

Then she heard a key being turned in the hall door. A moment later she was standing out there with Jørgen close to her side.

However, she fought down the temptation to immediately throw herself around his neck and shower him with questions. Despite the semidarkness in the hall, she had glimpsed the deep furrows that always appeared between Jørgen's eyebrows when he was preoccupied. Experience had taught her to avoid besetting him as soon as he appeared. Thus she simply stroked his cheek, helped him discard his coat, relieved him of his painting case, and placed it by the coatrack without so much as a peek at its contents, though her eyes burned to do just that. Then she led him, humming to herself, into the sitting room.

Jørgen, too, was quite taciturn. He slumped into his favorite armchair, rubbed his brow and hair with his neckerchief. "Dear God, I am thirsty," were his only weary words. Ursula went out to the kitchen and brought wine for him. Once she had returned and had poured it, she sat down on a stool by his feet, took his hand, and began to stroke it tentatively.

"And how are you, my love?" she finally began, given that he remained silent. "Have you had a good day?"

"Ah yes," he said as set the glass away from him and slewed the wine drops from his moustache with his lips and tongue. "I had quite an experience today. Magnificent in fact!"

"Do tell all! Where have you been all day?"

"Do you know... I am not even sure I know how to describe it. In the underworld. Where the real dregs seethe and boil. Where the new twentieth century is fermenting as we speak. In a word—the slum."

"The slum?"

"It was quite by chance, Ursula. I was just walking around with no real destination, and I thank my good lady Fortune that she led me there. Otherwise I may well have gone back to Denmark without ever having seen the only truly alive and enlightening thing in the whole of Rome. True... I have both read and heard often enough that it will be down here that the first sparks will erupt when the conflagration at last takes hold. But I only really understood that assertion this very day! Yes... it will be in precisely such plague-infested middens as I have seen today that the red bacillus will flourish. And most of the characters I saw lurking about down there look as though they will teach us a lesson one day. Not that you can see it on them. If you put the whole lot of them together, they wouldn't muster the lard quantity of a single self-satisfied Copenhagen merchant!"

"But you've been to other places, haven't you, darling?"

"Other places? I don't know what you mean. There was more than enough for me to see down there. You have to remember, this was the first time I've ever had the opportunity to look down into a real social 'abyss,' as these places are so poetically called. Because it is to our great misfortune in Denmark that we have no proletariat. That is why we have no freedom and probably will never achieve it. It doesn't matter how many laws we pass on paper!... My my, Ursula. If you had seen one gang of cutthroats I caught sight of in a backstreet drinking den—a proper ruffians' den. There they sat... five or six pale, malevolent bandits. They had dark, sunken blue rings around their eyes, as if they had all just escaped from a correction house. And as I walked past the open door, one of them sent me such a blood-vengeance look that it will stay with me forever! See... these are the things you have to experience yourself... with your own eyes... so as to grasp the huge stirrings that are underway in our times... especially when you emerge from such a den of iniquity like that into the Via del Corso and see all those Jew matrons and their fat backsides squashing those silk cushions on their blasted dining chairs!"

"So you haven't painted anything at all today?" said Ursula as she slipped his hand.

"Painted? Well, yes... Of course I painted!... But it's all rubbish. I don't truly *know* these people... No, I have to get back home to Denmark, Ursula! Time's up. There's no getting around it."

He jumped up from the chair and began to pace the floor. Backwards and forwards.

"There are all those strikes at home as well at the moment too. Child's play compared to events here and other places in the world, of course. But there's no getting around that. We are a Lilliput land! ... Does that mean we should just shrug our shoulders and do nothing? Never mind the fact that for us Danes, the struggle is more about how much extra butter or beer we can get inside us. A few more pennies in our pay packet. It's still a struggle. A clenched fist. A kick where it hurts for the ruling class, and—who knows?—maybe in the end it will unleash something ever greater. Oh, by the way... strange that my newspapers haven't come today. I'm dying to find out what is happening."

Ursula had sat motionless during this whole oration, as one gripped by a seizure. Bent forward and immersed in her own staring, corpse-like deliberations. With a start, she straightened, rose, and walked towards the desk, where the newspapers lay hidden. But she stopped halfway and changed her mind. With her head bowed and in silence, she went to Jørgen and eased her hand under his arm. Thus they traversed back and forth across the room, now completely bathed in moonlight. The only remaining shadows being in the furthest corners and below furniture.

"No, no... all this fancy talk and long-winded speeches about the need to keep the red flag's ideals and theories uppermost..." Jørgen continued, so caught up in his thoughts that he was unaware he spoke them aloud. "When it comes down to it... who are the ones that have risen up and thrown over the world order, time after time, from the first ever slave class onwards? The real revolutionaries? Precisely that gang of bloodless, narrow-gutted cellar rats, who would happily take all seven deadly sins on their conscience for a bottle of hooch! Ideals be damned... See... there you have our biggest problem in Denmark! Milksop liberals and do-gooders! Look at even our most fire-breathing socialists! Nothing but well-fed bourgeois courtesans. Respectable pork butchers and shopkeepers who are long reconciled to the Ten Commandments and the Lutheran catechism. Toytown burghers with money in the piggy bank. So of course they faint on the spot with moral conniptions when some deranged typographer shoots a button off a minister's overcoat, as happened recently! Fie, for shame. They sicken me more and more, those pettifoggers, who, oh yes, call for a revolution, but *en detail*, bit by bit. Dilettantes and philistines, actually. Quite happy with life, thank you very much, but need some radical cause to carry their careers, be that the labor movement, or women's suffrage. Up the republic! or other such empty blather. As if it made a jot of difference to prune a couple of twigs when the whole cursed tree is rotten to the core! . . . What are those gloves doing there on the table?"

"They are my father's. He was here early this afternoon."

"And he forgot his gloves . . ."

"Yes . . . my poor father . . . he has gotten so forgetful of late!"

"Forgetful? . . . Hmm," Jørgen muttered, but without continuing, for Ursula's sake. "That old scoundrel," he thought to himself. "I am on to his tricks and schemes! Now he uses every excuse to scuttle over here and sniff about early and late. Back at his black arts as soon as I'm gone. But I'll catch him out eventually!"

"Was there any special reason . . . for your father's visit?" he asked out loud.

"Actually, there was," Ursula replied. She was perched at the balcony door, wiping the dew off the windows with her handkerchief. "Oh, look, Jørgen! You have to look at this, darling."

"Yes, a clear, starry evening . . . But what were you saying? Your father has—?"

"Yes, Papa was up here to tell us about an evening jaunt out to Ponte Molle for this very night. The Seal Club is going to toast the arrival of spring in one of the gardens out there. It's an old custom that goes back decades, he says. He asked if we would like to come along."

"And you hopefully said no?"

Ursula threw an imploring look up at him, hastened to him, and pressed with all her heart against his arm.

"Jørgen," she said. "Be good tonight. I have missed you terribly all through this long day. I really want us to be happy with each other today . . . I need so much, so much, to show you how deep and intense my love is for you. Yes, you can just scold me and call it one of my notions . . . but just don't say no! . . . Say yes. Just this one time. Then I promise I will never plague you with such a request ever again. Is that all right? . . . Just say yes, Jørgen. I beg you so much."

Jørgen Hallager's brow furrowed and he looked down at his wife with a cold, distant stare.

"Now look here, Ursula . . . how many times have you promised me you would start getting a bit of sense, eh? Do you not think it's about time you did? I have also made clear to you already that I will not sit at the same table as those idiot Rome-posturers anymore. And let that be the end of it! . . . Toasting the arrival of spring . . . what utter rubbish. Aye, men! Toast spring and pretend your noses are not red with frostbite even with your winter furs and mountain gloves on! . . . I presume the mood sought for is High Romantic. The soaring of the spirit in the name of lofty poetics. Fie, Ursula! That you still want to make a fool of yourself, like that . . . And by the way . . . you are of course free to do as you please. Do what you want! But I am staying at home. I'm waiting for the post, anyway. I'd say the newspapers will come later this evening."

Ursula pulled her hand away from Jørgen's arm in the manner of one who has touched a hot coal. She then walked over to the writing desk, lifted the package of newspapers, and threw it onto the large table in the center of the room. There was no mistaking her disgust.

"There you are!" she said.

Jørgen looked at her in surprise for a moment. Then he went to the table, took the newspapers without any show of fuss, turned on the lamp, and took a seat in the nearby rocking chair.

"Right . . . let's see what's new from our Lilliput land," he said. Again as if nothing untoward had happened between himself and his wife. He spread out one of Copenhagen's main opposition newspapers in front of him. "And of course, yet another long spiel today by that hypocrite priest and his religious freethinking. A man who left his flock and ministry but still claims the cloth! Not worth reading . . . Religious freethinkers! Nonsense! Hermaphrodites is what I call them. Neither one thing nor the other. You'll see, Ursula. It won't be long before we have capitalist socialists and left-wing conservatives. A whole circus."

Ursula gave no answer. She had opened both wings of the balcony windows and their shutters, allowing the cold night air to invade the room. With her arms crossed over her chest, she stood leaning against the door frame, staring motionless across the moonlit city and farther and farther away. All the way out to the mountains in the far ethereal distance.

For several minutes, the room was silent.

"Good God!" Jørgen cried, leaning into the light from the lamp. Once more fully engrossed in his reading. "So our glorious Hr. Lønsted has been awarded the big travel grant. Did you hear that, Ursula?"

"Is it so strange?"

"Oh no . . . not in the least. Denmark's milksop culture personified. Grants and awards as acts of mercy . . . compensation for those to whom Mother Nature denied any gifts or talent whatsoever."

"Lønsted is actually a major talent. That's what Father says, anyway. And he should know. One needs to avoid showing all too obvious signs of envy."

Jørgen blanched behind his newspaper.

"Easy . . . easy now," he said to himself. He had sworn that he would be patient with Ursula. He understood only too well the fierce inner battle she was fighting at this time. Now that her delicate soul was striving upwards. Rising to new self-awareness and casting off the dead weight of fantasies and dreams that sought to drag her back down. Not for anything in the world did he wish to scare her. She would have time and space to anneal herself in those cleansing fires before embracing the morning air of the new dawn.

Thus he spoke to her in a calm, measured tone.

"You should close those doors now, dear . . . Ursula . . . don't stand there in that cold draft. You will catch a chill for certain, otherwise."

She gave no reply.

He waited a moment and then intervened again:

"Even if you don't carc about yourself, Ursula. Remember what we talked about the other day. Who knows? You might already need to take care for two people."

"I hope not."

Jørgen jumped up out of the chair. For a few moments, he stood still and fought down his hefty anger. Then he walked slowly to the balcony windows.

"Ur-sula!" he said. His voice soft. Almost pleading.

Her back and body twitched violently. A red blush fired her cheeks and her lips trembled. Then she suddenly turned right around and threw herself into him as a dam of convulsive sobbing broke from her.

"Hit me! hit me!" she cried. "I'm so rotten! I'm a bad, selfish person! ... Oh, oh! Just thrash me, will you! I deserve it!"

In vain Jørgen sought to calm her. First with gentle and then with stern and then finally with harsh words.

"Ursula! Ursula! Why can you never just take things in your stride? Where does all this high drama come from? ... You have completely lost the run of yourself. What the blazes is wrong with you?"

"I don't know... I don't know! I don't know who or what I am anymore! Oh, Jørgen, Jørgen—can you love a person so much that it makes you ill?"

"Ah, stop, Ursula. That's all just hot air and empty phrases. You need to start using a bit of common sense."

"Yes, yes, yes! I have to be good... try to be good... as long as you are not very vexed with me," she said, clinging to him as if in a mortal fear. "But I missed you so terribly today. It was never as bad as this. That is what gave me this turn. Nothing else. I swear... Oh, I am so tired, so very tired."

Her head slumped down onto his chest.

"Yes, and there you see what happens, my love!" Jørgen said. "All this comes from that blasted moonlight hocus-pocus and poetic reverie palaver. You are literally shaking like a leaf... Can't you see for yourself that you are much much better than that? ... Will you promise me faithfully, Ursula, that this is the last time? Will you?"

"Yes, yes... I will! I promise... I'm so ashamed now."

"But will you keep that promise this time?" He drove her on now. Fired up by her total capitulation. "And will you promise me to throw all those who seek to hold you back down those damn stairs. I think your father has been running over here at every turnabout when I have been elsewhere. What exactly has he said to you? Is it him that put—"

"No. It's me! I swear... It's just me!"

"Well, then. This time... be sure and keep to your word and pull that whole temple of false gods to the ground! Can't you smell its stink of mildew? How its rotten decay is poisoning our happy marriage? Blow it all to kingdom come, Ursula! Be brave. Be steadfast..."

"Yes, yes—I promise I will do that, Jørgen.—But I am so tired, so very tired... I can't think straight anymore... oh, look at all those many stars!"

With that, she collapsed, senseless, into his arms.

5

AS JØRGEN HALLAGER had complained many times, it was indeed the case that a rough-and-ready osteria housed in the Baths of Diocletian had been chosen as a favored venue by Rome's Scandinavian colony that winter. These gigantic ruins, whose gray-green mossy walls and sloping roofs loomed like some fossilized mammoth over the modern city's skeletal, matchstick constructions, had over the centuries evolved into a vast Noah's Ark type emporium. Every human activity imaginable—both wholesome and unwholesome—was pursued in the depths of the many uniformly built bathrooms, which ran in an unbroken sequence right around the building, rather like individual cells in a huge beehive: craftsmen and small traders, barbers and victualers, hospitals and museums; a corner had even been found within these old pagan walls for a church. All alike sharing this vast space with the countless birds, rats, lizards, bats, and similar creepers, crawlers, and flitters darting in and out of the multitude of cracks and crevices in the roofs and walls.

Signor Francesco's *cucina* was a sizable whitewashed, high-vaulted room whose interior would remind any rural Dane, at least, of the crepuscular interior of a Danish village church. However, the inhabitants were precisely those who might constitute the less distinguished inhabitants of a Noah's Ark. All around the coarse benches—where swarthy railway workers and farm laborers from the Campagna in their goatskin jerkins wolfed their *salsiccia* sausages—chickens and hens strode about, frantically pecking at the crumbs and other debris falling between the rows of work boots. Atop the tables themselves, hefty tabby cats sat or flexed their velvet backs and watched lazily as mottled pigeons flapped and lithe swallows zipped through the smoke-filled air. Signor Francesco himself stood like a chattering parrot by the large open fireplace, dressed in shirtsleeves and a blue paper chef's hat as a nod to hygiene. Meanwhile his *moglie*—a grand diva-like Roman matron with blue-black hair and a pair of dangling donkey-shoe-sized silver earrings—performed waitress duties, the still-breastfeeding baby in her arms being no hindrance. Strangest of all in this hectic zoo was the Noah's Ark bridge deck itself; a mighty-timbered box, which, like a traditional suspended food pantry with netted windows to keep flies at bay, hung high in the ceiling and was connected to the floor by way of a steep chicken-coop ladder. Up here were the family bedrooms; and of an evening, when the lamps were lit and the room packed with diners, a black-haired little boy in nothing but his bare shirt would appear at the top of the ladder, peering avidly down through the dense clouds of tobacco; an appearance that always provoked applause and rapturous cries from the assembled Scandinavians who practiced an almost religious worship of "the little angel up in the clouds."

One evening at the beginning of March, this hostelry was the scene of uproar and scandal. For the whole evening, the room had been crowded with people. Men and women came and went in loud voices and gesticulations. The normally lethargic regular customers, meanwhile, were to be seen and heard screaming into each other's faces at their many small tables. One struggled to hear speech or hear oneself think in this bedlam. Only the Nordic contingent, which was benched at a long table at the very end of the vast room, was unusually subdued in its conversation. At this table, the straw-encased wine bottles stood almost untouched and a somber aspect prevailed over their normally vivacious demeanor.

Earlier that day, a dreadful incident had occurred. Anarchist agitators had once again carried out an attack, and this time in Rome itself. As spring made its flamboyant and joy-inducing entry into the Holy City and Mother Nature wooed its inhabitants to thoughts of feast and brotherly love, this reckless band of murderers had emerged from one of its impenetrable lairs and had, by way of dynamite blasts, violently shaken the people from their spring-infused jocundity. A police station near the Via del Corso was blown up. Five people were badly injured and a child killed; such was the import of these terror-tidings that flew wailing through the streets like an unexpected storm that erupts just before sunset . . . precisely at that hour when the city's many foreign worshippers stepped out from galleries and museums after a day's immersion in beauty and splendor, or were returning home from excursions in the surrounding hills, laden with fresh young flowers and intoxicated by the newborn heat and the mystical beauty of nature. They met a populace in uproar and tumult. The wildest rumors of further conspiracies and outrages to come. Even the precise wording of threatening letters from other imagined gangs of anarchist plotters raced from mouth to mouth. All the streets around Via del Corso roiled and foamed as one monstrous tide of people . . . and the waves from this troubled sea rushed into Signor Francesco's usually tranquil wine-hostelry.

The Scandinavian colony had assembled in full muster, so to speak. Outrage and fear always being the best marshaling sergeant; just as a thunderstorm will drive cattle in a field to flock together. At the head of the table sat the patrician Supreme Court Senior Counsel Hoskjær, his ruddy features further emblazoned by his awareness of the profundity of the occasion. He was further adorned by his wife, a lush and striking Titian-type blonde, who, in spite of her thirty-eight years, had anguished the heart of more than one of the young artists seeking inspiration in these southern climes. Councilor of State Hr. Branth was also present, though now very much a shadow of his former self. Next to him was Thorkild Drehling, who had not long returned from his travels in the south of Italy where he had engaged in a consciously high-minded odyssey across a desolate mountain range; his only company being a couple of goatherds. He had, during this time, become even more serious and reserved than before. Drehling remained in his seat all evening, leaning back against the rough wall, his arms folded across his chest and taking no part whatsoever in the conversation. But for all that, his dark, melancholy eyes rarely strayed away from the other end of the table, where Jørgen and Ursula had been given seats.

It was Jørgen Hallager himself who had proposed the gathering this evening, because—as he said privately—he wanted to see how a cheery seal colony would react to a dynamite outrage. Though it is true that his decision to absent himself from the Ultima fraternity and their soirees had not been a source of sorrow for his compatriots. The arrogant mockery in which he at all times engaged, and above all his behavior towards his aging father-in-law, who was now on the verge of mental collapse and despair, had inflamed the mood against Hallager still further.

Given the general mood of dejection that prevailed among the company, Senior Counsel Hoskjær felt it incumbent upon himself to say a few consoling, but also encouraging, words. Thus he straightened his long back, smoothed his dinner jacket, and patted his graying hair, or what was left of it to the sides and rear. He then adjusted his veneration-inducing gold spectacles, struck his glass with no little force, and stood up.

He began by relating an anecdote. With great verbal dexterity and deep engagement, he told the story of one of his friends from his student days, a certain Hr. Sørensen, who was so fretful regarding his health that he annually swallowed an entire pharmacy and could never hear talk of a new ointment, laxative pill, or miracle elixir without having to try it immediately. This same Sørensen had, at one stage, been so anxious about his breathing that he hardly dared to breathe at all. And though he was an otherwise sturdy and unusually well-built man in the prime of his life, he saw sickness and death approaching him at every street corner. Once, when a few cases of smallpox broke out in Copenhagen, he woke up one morning and, to his utter terror, discovered three red dots on his hand. Half dead with fear, he asked to be stretchered from his bed to a waiting carriage below and driven to the hospital; where, however, his extreme concern was dismissed with a reminder that a hospital would hardly worry about bites from bedbugs.

This former fellow student, Hoskjær continued, often came to his mind in these new times, when so many people, both old and young, but most of all the young, had a strange urge to seek out the dark side of life and view the world as one big pestilential vale of tears. He simply could not fathom this despondency. "Did not the sky shine just as bright and blue now as in the halcyon days of our fathers? Were the forests and trees any less green? Did violets smell less sweet? Had love, starlight, and the nightingale's enchanting evensong vanished with the advent of the mail coach and the postman's horn and official undertakers' carriages? Not in the least, ladies and gentlemen! But we have—like poor Hr. Sørensen—become sickly... obsessed with medicaments, cures, and potions in the vain hope of curing all life's ills. In other words, in our anxiety for the public and common good, we have made ourselves hostage to society's intellectual snake-charmers and quack merchants, who with all manner of promises and miracle solutions have poisoned society's previously healthy blood-circuits and destroyed its nervous system. It is here, my learned friends, that we find the source of all these new ideological strands that so disturb the social contract and the body politic and have bedeviled us for so long now. Here the source of these hideous outbreaks and eruptions, which, for example today, have filled all right-thinking men with disgust. But—and here is my point—one must be careful not to overestimate the significance of such irregularities, let alone allow them to intimidate us. For despite his own foibles and notions, my good Hr. Sørensen—after all—had supreme confidence in society's institutions and constitution. Our precious civic society has been built over many centuries on massive and unshakable foundations, which have defied much greater storms of fanaticism than the one that has swept over our countries just recently. It would therefore be extremely naïve, indeed a gross overreaction, in fact a sin, to even imagine that these occasional disturbances might dislodge so much as a particle of that proud, immovable edifice.

"And yet... and yet," he concluded, "it is only natural that on a day like this we think of our distant fatherland with particular fondness and emotion. Let us hope that what has happened down here today will at least have one positive outcome . . . and that is to open our Nordic eyes to those 'miracle men'—be they of the communist red or anarchist black variety—who believe they are the possessors of a magic cure for society's ills and perversely reject the obvious truth . . . that only through steady, patient development can progress be made and true equality be established. Let us hope that all right-thinking men—be they of the right or of the left, rich or poor—will henceforth put aside all those paltry, meaningless quarrels and stand unbreakable, shoulder to shoulder, in defense of the wholesome, thoughtful, and calm well-being of our people. So with that and Denmark's honor always in mind, ladies and gentlemen, I ask you to rise for this toast: God save the king and our dear fatherland."

"Hear!—Hear!—Hear!" came the cry from all sides.

The speech had exactly the effect Senior Counsel Hoskjær had intended. All rose as one and lifted their glasses high. The red flush of fervor on their cheeks:

"God save the king and our dear fatherland!"

Only Jørgen Hallager remained seated. He did not even deign to touch his glass. However, most of the company pretended not to notice this demonstration. As if by tacit agreement, they not only completely ignored him, but competed with each other to offer the biggest smile or nod and supportive shouts across the table to Ursula, who had risen with the others. In fact not just risen with the others, but clinked her glass with those around her with a conspicuous zeal, though she could not possibly have missed the fact that her husband had remained seated.

Jørgen tried his best to smile. But on this occasion, he was far less successful at maintaining that cold-blooded self-control which, almost more than his gross insults, had made him a figure of disgust and despised by this fraternity. It was with great relish, therefore, that people around the table noticed how Jørgen Hallager had grown visibly pale and stiff.

In the meantime, a diminutive gentleman of a most amiable deportment and mien had knocked on his glass. And once all Seal Club adherents were seated again, this same man bowed deeply to all sides and inquired as to whether he might beg permission to add a few brief remarks to the Supreme Court counsel's most gracious and edifying speech. The speaker was none other than the poet Folehave, a guest at Ursula Branth's marriage to Jørgen Hallager.

"As Hr. Senior Counsel expresses it so well," Folehave began, "society in our times reveals itself as the image and epitome of widespread lethargy. It seems that everywhere one looks a sad decline, a fateful decay, is spreading rapidly. And everywhere, in all countries, this disease exhibits the same symptoms: weariness and despondency in the elderly, a sluggish and spiritless youth, and in general a petulant and unsettled populace. The cause of this collapse gradually becomes clear to all those not already blinded by political partisanship. It is due, we see, to a misconception of what life's true, fundamental values actually are, or—as the senior counsel so brilliantly and tellingly expressed it—a hugely exaggerated concern for material possessions and well-being, leading to indifference to, even downright contempt for, those timeless metaphysical treasures, which neither dry rot nor rust can ever touch."

"Hear!—Hear!" came the approving cries from his audience.

"In other words, ladies and gentlemen!" Folehave continued, strengthening his voice, "this is the diagnosis, as we approach the momentous end to this century... this is the pestilence that has infected our society and laid waste to everything. It is nothing other than a spiritual Black Death... What we are suffering from is that desolate, materialistic view of life that has been so virulent in the arts, sciences, literature, and politics for more than fifty years."

"That... is all lies," Jørgen mumbled, half to himself.

"I beg your pardon?" Hr. Folehave broke off, as everybody else turned and shot baleful stares towards the far end of the table.

"I am telling you that all that is base slander," Jørgen repeated, this time with his full voice.

Senior Counsel Hoskjær rose and, summoning all his majesty, said:

"As our fraternity's elected president, I must request quite firmly that people desist from that kind of rude and indecent interruption.

Such behavior will not under any circumstances be tolerated here. I do beg you, Hr. Folehave, to continue your speech and simply ignore such interference."

"Ah yes, um, many thanks, Senior Counsel... So, er... as I was saying," the poet resumed, still struggling to regather his threads, to the background of further ripples of indignation against Jørgen Hallager, "yes, the disease has been diagnosed, my friends, and its cause is now known. The issue now, of course, is the cure. For we Ultima Thule folk, so happy to be here in precious Rome at this present time and to be daily surrounded and enthralled by the pure and vivifying *Geist* of momentous bygone times... for us, I say, the treatment and cure cannot be doubted. For it is to be obtained in the profound tranquility of great antiquity. Yes... in the soaring, beauty-intoxicated, heavenward flight that was the Renaissance, we see the path we must take. The path that leads us away from the wallowing in deep and ignominious misery we see today. Only then can we dare hope for an intellectual and spiritual renewal of humanity; for the rebirth of broad contentment and joy, when the gaze of the people is once again lifted away from the sad desolation of everyday life; when our longings and dreams can rise and join the racing clouds and heavenly vault—"

"Bravo, sir!" Jørgen Hallager protested, again in a loud voice. "Just like Harlequin who sends Pierrot the fool off to look at the starry sky so he can run off with buxom Columbine. A whole damn pantomime!"

The senior counsel shot to his feet.

"Now you really must hold your tongue, sir!" he screamed, blood-red with indignation. "We will not tolerate your brazen behavior a moment longer."

"And I will no longer tolerate this man standing there and spouting nonsense, because he is too much of an imbecile to understand the greatness of the times in which he lives."

"Oh my word, did you hear that?... That is outrageous. I say, what a ruffian... Complete lout!... Throw him out on his ear!" came the cries from the whole gathering. Hr. Folehave, meanwhile, turned towards Hallager and with an attempt at superior irony cried out:

"My apologies, Hr. Hallager. But is it your good self, or I, that has the floor, sir?"

"It is me!" Jørgen Hallager roared, striking the table with his fist as he stood up. His face grew ashen in an instant and he paid no heed to the storm of bitter taunts that sought to drown his words. "So, is that the height of it?" he continued. "Are we going to let a two-bit writer like him stand there and spew his filthy mockery over an age which he'd better be thanking his God he lived to see... an age whose deeds history will one day emblazon with a golden glow and which posterity will pronounce as the greatest ever century of mankind!... Yes, just scream! Just roar and protest all you want! All of you clowns!... But then name me a century in which such huge progress has been made as ours! Name one! Yes, the Renaissance is always thrown up. Time after time! As if a few paintings and a scattering of fairy-tale comedies count for greatness! Yes, bark like dogs! Be my guest. But I am telling you all... that none of that whole concoction has as much value for mankind as a single one of the scientific discoveries in our age, and that's before we speak of its social reforms! Even that Lutheran Reformation that is spoken of by Danes with such awe and reverence. What is *that* in comparison with the educational initiatives produced by the social and political movements of our age, which are now bearing fruit among the broad and galvanized masses?"

"Fruit? Ha! Oh yes, such lovely fruit!" they screamed at him. "Communists... strikes... riots... anarchists!... Yes, the anarchists! What about the anarchists, eh?"

"Very well, Your Majesties. Let us discuss that very fruit..." Hallager was by now obliged to use the full force of his booming voice to shout down the wall of catcalls. "The raising of the great social questions; the political agitation in our times; the organizing of our great armies of workers... It is precisely these great feats that are the finest and proudest triumphs of our century. A masterpiece far better than any Renaissance work. Why...? Because the like of it has never been seen before in the whole of world history. What you are all staring in the face is the final, victorious battle that has broken the shackles of slavery that held mankind, toiling and groaning, in bondage for thousands of years! Just wait, my esteemed ladies and gentlemen. You will all soon hear and see much more of this freedom's army."

"Yes. Bombs and murder! ... Anarchists! Anarchists!" came the cries from all sides. "Stop avoiding the point, Hallager!"

"Of course, the anarchists! And what? And what? Yes, yes ... the anarchists too are playing their welcome part. Surely the commotion you are all raising here tonight proves my point ... ? What are a few lives lost here and there if it opens closed ears and minds, like your own, to the millions of screams of the downtrodden and oppressed?"

It was no longer possible to hear Jørgen Hallager's words in the whole cacophony. All the resentment and disgust that had been building up against him during the winter now vented its spleen. Most of the "colony" had jumped up from the long benches. A quite young, fantastically garbed lady shouted and thrust her twisted face forward. "I could spit in your face, you utter wretch." Two other ladies had rushed to Ursula, who, for a moment, seemed about to faint. Her father, poor State Councilor Branth, was also the subject of great attention and sympathy. The poet Folehave was now entirely forgotten, never mind the fact he was still standing there with glass in hand, endlessly repeating his superbly ironic put-down:

"My apologies, Hr. Hallager. But is it your good self, or I, that has the floor, sir?"

Senior Counsel Hoskjær now completely abandoned any attempt at bringing things to order, and for a moment complete disarray threatened. Only when the indigenous patrons of the trattoria began to take an interest in the disorder—in particular when the word "anarchists" was roared repeatedly—did he find it indisputably necessary to assert himself, more in the manner of a common parade-ground sergeant. Summoning all the power of his foghorn lungs, he vanquished all noise, declared the court in recess and that the public gallery should be cleared, but not without reminding of the need to respect local sensitivities and to depart from the room quietly, quickly, and in good order, which admonishment was immediately obeyed. Though there were still those who fired hefty insults at "the despicable agitator" as they left the room. Very soon, only Jørgen and Ursula remained at the deserted table.

State Councilor Branth and Thorkild Drehling walked home together through the now empty and quiet streets. Hr. Branth had specifically asked Hr. Drehling to accompany him. And the old man did not hesitate in taking the young artist's arm, as he stumbled at every other step, spoke almost constantly, and openly shed tears as they walked along. Living proof that this highly respected dignitary, who had previously always been so restrained, so correct—yes, punctilious to a fault (or as Jørgen Hallager used to say about him: "Fussy with an ass in it") had in recent months completely lost all sense of *comportment* and could seldom be in friendly company without pouring his troubled heart out.

"My poor, poor child!" Hr. Branth intoned over and over, thunderstruck as he was by this new scandal and having lost all composure.—"What shall I do, eh? How shall I save her from being devoured by that monster?... He will kill her in the end! I know it! He will kill her, I tell you... ah dear God..."

Thorkild Drehling sought to calm and reassure him, though he himself had been shaken to the core by the evening's events.

"Try not to take your son-in-law's utterances too literally, sir. I know him of old and it is just his way to use dramatic and extreme language," Drehling said, without really meaning any of it. "Do you remember, Hr. Branth, that you yourself once described him as a monomaniac... a child of our political times?"

"Yes, indeed! Ah dear... a child of our wretched times! Actually a child of our own homegrown, intemperate, unrestrained, rabble-rousing conspirators, whom the good Lord will one day punish with His mighty hand... And a child, of course, of his own father... that criminal schoolteacher over there in the back of the wild beyond and hostile coast. Did you not know his father, Hr. Drehling? Another anarchist... was he not?"

"I am not really sure, sir," Drehling replied with no little evasion. "I have only heard that on one occasion Jørgen's father fought with his superiors and was therefore banished to a poorly paid teaching post in the far western extreme of the North Sea coast. We might therefore forgive any collapse into sloth. I believe he also died in great destitution."

"Destitution! There you have it! The mighty hand of God! This is what that devil will face eventually! Thus does God punish disobedience! . . . And Hallager is his disobedient father's son! Did you not once tell me that he has always admired his father? Yes, actually worshipped him . . . literally?"

"I think rather that Jørgen perhaps sees his role in life as being his father's avenging angel . . ."

"Yes, of course! That is what I am saying. Revenge. Hatred. Murder! The dark spirit of our age. You have him, Hr. Drehling! He does not understand mercy and forbearance. Sees it as weakness. Oh no! Revenge. Hatred. Murder. The only answer."

They had now reached the hotel where the state councilor had kept rooms since Ursula's marriage. Back then, he had given up his private residence, as it had been his intention to go back to Denmark fairly quickly. But week after week, month after month, he had postponed his departure. He could simply not bring himself to abandon his daughter in her hour of need.

The state councilor now urged Hr. Drehling to partake of a nightcap up in his rooms. For as he put it himself, he did not care to be left alone at that moment in his anxiety and despair.

"I say, Hr. Drehling. Would you like to enjoy some final refreshments in my rooms? Do come! . . . I was not really able to thank you properly for the happy moments you gifted me earlier today," he said. This was in reference to a visit Hr. Branth had made in the afternoon, along with his daughter Ursula, to Hr. Drehling's atelier to view his new works. "I have always said, sir, that you would once again find the right path! Come, we can discuss this further upstairs."

But Thorkild Drehling made his excuses; citing fatigue and the lateness of the hour. He was too preoccupied with his own thoughts and certain resolutions he had made to continue what was in effect the same conversation over and over. Thus he shook the state councilor's hand and bade him a heartfelt farewell. Moments later Drehling was making his way along the now completely deserted and hushed streets of Rome.

His onward journey led him past the church of the Santissima Trinità dei Monti and its elevated position above the Piazza di Spagna. The same church and its bells that had rung out his departure from Rome months before. He tarried here a while. Staring out over the city below him, all wreathed in night mist. Out over that same panorama of a myriad fairy-tale steeples, above which the heavens were revealed as a vast canvas, increasingly dark-blue in tone and dappled with bright, golden stars. In the depths beneath him, the famous fountain murmured and whispered in the darkness. Here and there the sound of rolling carriages and the footsteps of lone pedestrians could be heard.

At this heightened moment, he made a solemn promise to himself. The very next day, he would break decisively with his former comrade and mentor. This was the real reason, he knew, he had returned to Rome. Not a day longer would he waste in removing the last remnants of a past life as an artist that weighed on him like a great shame!... Oh that he could have been so blind! How, in heaven's name, could he have allowed himself to be so heedlessly seduced by this berserker, who constantly rushed headlong into any and every situation and trampled and destroyed all the radiant, delicate flowers that resided in the human soul. All the sacred feelings of the heart! How could he possibly have involved himself in this insane pursuit of the phantom they called collective freedom! Freedom for the masses as freedom for man! When each man, until the world's absolute end, would remain enslaved and engaged with his own individual passions. Each individual man, who from cradle to grave struggled daily under the heavy yoke of his own fierce ambitions, his ire, his self-love! Which law or social regulation can provide relief for the torments of unrequited love! What mass movement can ease the anxiety of a lonely heart! The bitter affliction that is a devotion denied!

"Ah, Ursula—my dear, beloved Ursula!"

Her translucent face came to him in the dark night... he gazed at her glorious aura. Her eyes so clear and resplendent in that vista.

The proud way she had defied her executioner that very evening as she lifted her glass to the others! Was there still hope? Did she still have the strength and courage to break her chains? And did he, Thorkild Drehling, have the courage of his newfound convictions? Did he dare to give her a helping hand?... In fact to rescue her? Did he too have that courage?

In the depths of this still night, the fountain responded with an endless leaden murmuring. To him, it sounded for all the world like the lonely, despairing cry of a distraught woman.

6

THE NEXT morning at sunrise, Jørgen partook of his usual morning walk through Trastevere and along the right bank of the River Tiber. His habit of rising early had begun when he moved to Copenhagen, where the first blasts from docks, mill and factory horns and hooters, to signal the morning shift change, would rouse him from his slumbers. He welcomed this siren call to work and the chance it gave him to get out and observe the fascinating drama that a waking city always meant for him. He would spend hours in the gray and foggy winter mornings wandering around the backstreets, watching the workers as they made for the shipyards or workshops, sandwich boxes under their arms and invariably a pocket flask of schnapps protruding from a side pocket. He loved the way the factory girls walked two by two and arm in arm, always late it seemed, hurrying together, still pale and drawn from the adventures of the night before. The thickset and bustling newspaper women with their hands on the huge piles of papers. Then the wraithlike, red-nosed children who, still half-asleep and shivering in the cold, dragged themselves to the coal dealer with buckets too big for them.

He and Ursula had not exchanged a single word since the events of the previous evening. On the way home from Francesco's, he had tried to strike a cheerful, conciliatory tone, but she had clearly not wished to offer any reply, and they soon both lapsed into silence. During the night, several times, he had heard her sobbing into her pillow, but on each occasion, as soon as she noticed he was awake, she had fought down her sobs and lain perfectly still.

Poor Ursula! It pained him to the quick, that she was still suffering so much. But it could not be helped! It was now a case of their seeing it through to the end. She had obviously now reached the critical point. The battle would soon be fought out, and she would emerge fully purged and tempered. Strong and free!

When he returned home, the breakfast table had been set as usual in front of the large plants. Ursula had risen and toileted and was now standing outside on the sun-kissed balcony in her white morning dress. A Roman silk shawl was thrown about her shoulders. She did not turn around on his entering and barely answered his good morning.

"Well then, tea and toast," he said in a neutral tone. "Come and sit down, Ursula!"

"I don't want anything."

"I see...what a shame! Does your husband really have to eat alone?...Oh, come on...try and get something inside you. Going hungry for so long will do you no good whatsoever."

She gave no answer.

Jørgen threw a quick scrutinizing glance at her. Then he nodded to himself, as if resolved in some decision, and sat down at the table.

On his plate was a postcard from Thorkild Drehling. It read:

> As you have expressed a desire to see my new works before they are packed and sent to Denmark for the Spring Exhibition, I would ask that you visit my atelier tomorrow morning, preferably before 11 o'clock. Should I be absent, you can get the key from the janitor. I am actually coming up to Purificazione tomorrow at lunchtime and hope to see you at home. I will bring with me an envelope with some postcards, which I found lying on my table after your wife and father-in-law's visit this afternoon. One of them must have presumably left them behind.
>
> Th. D.

Jørgen placed the card to one side and began to eat.

"There's word from Drehling,", he said after a while. "I'm to go up and view his new paintings this very morning. I'm curious to see the final results of all his time down here. By the way, he says that you and your father were over there with him yesterday... you didn't tell me. Spill the beans, Ursula! What are these new masterpieces like? He has been so mysterious all winter."

"You will soon see," came her terse reply.

He shot another quizzical glance at her. Only now did he really study her face. How pale she looked! How dark the shadows under her eyes had become. Easy now! Say nothing... don't buckle, Hallager! No backsliding!

Out on the balcony, Ursula turned and entered the sitting room. Her movements were slow. She walked back and forth across the floor a couple of times and then sat down in the armchair that was at a distance from the table.

"Will you tell me," she said, "did you mean all the points you made last night... at Francesco's?"

"What things?" Jørgen asked with feigned surprise.

"All that about politics and the anarchists... and all the rest of it."

Jørgen's brow furrowed deeply.

"Do you think I usually joke about such things?"

"Oh no. Of course... it's your religion. You have none other!"

She got up again and resumed her pacing of the room.

"Look here, Ursula," Jørgen said out loud a little later, "it seems obvious to me that you have been very unhappy lately... that you are not enjoying our stay anymore. And the only reason I have remained here is for your sake. So now we really should go ahead and do just that. Go home. There are other pressing reasons too, that make it a good idea. In fact, most necessary. So I say we go back to Denmark next week."

"Go back?"

"Yes... let us say Tuesday. The sooner, the better. The air down here obviously affects you... or maybe it's the company we have to keep. I don't know. But let's put an end to all this and make our minds up. We travel on Tuesday and that's that."

Ursula, who had stopped midstride to listen to him, went to the window, where she stood and looked out.

"Do what you want," she said finally. "But I'm not traveling anywhere."

"You what . . . ? You are not traveling?"

"Not with you!"

Jørgen flung his napkin to the table.

"Have you lost your mind? You don't really know what you are saying, Ursula!"

He shot up from his chair, and pushed it away with great force.

"Yes, just hit me! Beat me black-and-blue," she screamed, as she turned to him with flashing eyes. "Why just threaten? After all, you are the great supporter of raw violence! The great defender of murderers! Why don't you just kill me on the spot? That would set a commotion going and open closed ears to the screams of the oppressed, wouldn't it?"

"Shut your damn mouth, woman . . . because if you are not careful you will go too far . . . I will no longer put up with your constant criticism and undermining of me! . . . Now . . . I am going to go out. I hope you have come to your senses by the time I get back."

He was barely in the street outside when he began to regret his impetuosity. It was the first time ever that the fury of which he was capable had unleashed itself upon her. Should he go back right away? . . . "No, absolutely not! What are you thinking of, Hallager! Devil take it all! Can man and wife not speak from the heart to each other?!" . . . And anyway, all this would soon be over, and Ursula would then understand him. Even thank him. Precisely because he had not let her down in her fateful hour, but rather had avoided false pity and let her endure that rite of passage to its victorious conclusion!

It was not long before he stood outside a large, monastery-like building, in which Thorkild Drehling had his rooms. Thorkild was not at home; but the janitor—an old one-eyed man who had obviously been informed of Jørgen's possible coming—took a massive bundle of rusty keys from the vestibule wall and with hand gestures alone, for he spoke not a word, bade Jørgen follow him. First, they crossed a narrow courtyard that reeked of damp and was lined with green mold, the walls otherwise dominated by a weathered stone basin;

from there down through a low and dark basement corridor, across another courtyard, and then up over a brick bridge adorned on both sides by an orange-colored trellis. Finally, they stood in front of a tower-like building, in whose lower story Drehling's atelier was to be found.

The atelier itself was a large, imposing room whose blank walls carried a cool greenish tinge from the adjacent garden. It was on the wall opposite a high curved window that all the new paintings were hung. The window's curtain had been drawn aside, so that the full light of day could illuminate all of them equally.

Jørgen sat astride a chair in the middle of the floor and began to study the paintings.

In all, there were around a dozen paintings, mostly works in progress, and some quite small sketches. Common to them all was a vivacity of color, indeed a joy-taking in color, that would surprise anyone used to viewing Thorkild Drehling as a faithful imitator of Jørgen Hallager's forceful but strictly subdued painting style and palette. But even more surprising than the technical execution were the narratives conveyed in these pictures. For here were fantasies, dream-inspired images, strange and enigmatic visions, thrown onto the canvas with an almost deliberately provocative contempt for the iron laws of reality or probable sequence. Here was a fabulous, primordial forest shrouded in a dense lilac haze, in which a herd of large gray mythical creatures wandered and grazed at will. And there was a small patch of dark-blue sky, under which a flock of wild, snow-white swans exploded into flight. A third painting depicted a deep valley with an emerald-green lake as its inverted eye, which eye was surrounded by black cypress trees. A faun and a nymph frolicked by the lakeshore. The largest painting, and also the closest to completion, depicted a scene from the "Agnete and the Merman" legend of Danish folk ballad renown. On a wide, wind-scoured, deserted beach, with a dark, glowering sky above it, the ocean heaves its vast waves to shore. Behind a huge rock, out in the wildest part of the surging surf, the figure of the Merman can be seen. He is lifting himself up out of the water by one of his brawny arms and is staring beyond the barren dunes at the small wind-blasted church in the far distance. The very place where his Agnete has disappeared from view. His free hand he is sweeping to one side in apparent annoyance, as if to ward off his little son who, free of all cares, is cavorting atop the surf and blowing a conch. The Merman's bearded mouth is slightly open and this gives his face an expression of primitive savagery. However, his large round fish-eyes radiate an infinite goodness, and a quiet and patient longing more akin to a faithful hound. The confident and reassured air of a trusting husband. "Agnete will doubtless come," he seems to be saying to himself. "It is true, I have waited here three days and nights. But never would she deceive me. Be it this day. This night. Tomorrow. She will surely come in the end."

Jørgen had allowed his gaze to roam from painting to painting... and all the while his face gradually drained of color. Finally, he nodded to himself and muttered: "Et tu, Brute, my son!" So his suspicions had been correct! So this was the well-kept secret! Plotting betrayal and treachery! That was why Thorkild had vanished from Rome and taken such great pains to hide himself away. From him and the other comrades!... The others? What others? Were there any more left? Even the stalwart Rasmus had been mentioned in the last dispatches as having succumbed to the new fantasy-and-dream pestilence! Each new newspaper delivery brought news of new renegades, new defeats, new devastation wrought by the forces of reaction, a great host of sickly phantoms abroad once more!

He stood up, of a sudden, and pulled at his collar as if he were suffocating. He felt that he was overwhelmed... entombed... the stench of corpses, mold, and dead toads seeming to fill his nostrils. Without any deference to the one-eyed man who had remained standing at the door with his rusty bundle of keys, he pushed out both wings of the window and shouted in a loud voice:

"Air—air—air!"

Then a thought struck him. Ursula had been here yesterday and seen these very paintings... yet she had not wished to discuss them this morning. Was this where the explanation was to be found for her strange behavior since yesterday? Of course! Now he understood everything! This stinking emanation from these newly opened phantasm-and-spookery catacombs had polluted her senses and led her astray once more! . . . So she was no further on! Stronger she was not . . . All her valiant struggles and despair, her bitter cries in the night . . . all for nothing!

"Ursula . . . Ursula," he breathed.

Was the battle lost then? Was this great hope, too, destroyed? Was even this sliver of light in the overall darkness truly now extinguished for him . . . the first, in fact the only, bright ray that ever illuminated his life path? So be it! Then he would just have to start over and fight the eternal life-or-death struggle on his own, as the enemy plunged existence itself into darkness all around him! Nor could he even complain. He deserved this fate. Oh yes . . . for a moment, his resolve had weakened . . . he had been a fool . . . yes, he too, Jørgen Hallager, a dreamer . . . a blasted love-fool . . . just like all the others. He saw the whole canvas so clearly now. Slowly, slowly, bit by bit, he had fallen prey to the general evisceration of manliness that was abroad in this new age. What had his original affiliation with Ursula meant for him? Yes . . . a cavorting in a sensual no-man's-land. A pleasing of his vanity. In fact a snare . . . a battle trophy for his enemies! And now what? . . . He could not, he had to admit, think of her without his heart bulging and beating faster. Could not be away from her for even one single hour without having to fight the urge to rush home. He was her dog. Her slave. While she—! Yes she . . . Ah, fie, for shame . . . that folk simply could not stop believing that fairy-tale dross about the power of love to unite souls! . . . No no . . . Spite. Bile. Eternal struggle. That was it. Antagonism. Mutual hatred! Mutual revenge! That was what fired and welded things together! Kept them bright!

At the door the old man rattled his bundle of keys to signal his impatience. Jørgen understood the gesture, threw a couple of soldi into his cap and began the journey homewards. He was in no hurry.

On his way back, he stopped for a moment and looked out over the city. His huge fists bunched instinctively in his pockets. He thought of all the good artists who had, for so long, come to this devil's pit—sound and strong of soul and mind they had been. Yet once here they were lured to catastrophe by falsehoods and dancing phantasms. The Fata Morgana that then ensnared them, floundering like trapped flies in her mesmeric glittering web. What was it again that Rome was called in the Book of Revelation? The Whore of Babylon, was it? Yes. And nothing had changed! From this very citadel . . . from this hallowed *territorium*, the decadence had spread across the whole world. It was from here that myriad bright minds had been corrupted to dark, feverish fantasies. To gargoyle visions. To that whole frenzied orgy of sycophancy that sucked the marrow of human will and laid waste to the world. But revenge was at hand. The revenge of calm, cool reality! Judgment pronounced on it, tormented, starved, and impoverished like no other land in Christendom, this City of Miracles lay devastated and fought its death struggle. And so it would lie in death's straits and suffer all the torments of annihilation, until—finally—that new dawn broke and crushed its legion of idols to dust. Then and only then could it rise again.

7

WHEN JØRGEN got home around lunchtime, the portly janitress told him that a visitor—a *signore*—had just gone up before him. On the way up the countless stairs, he also heard someone being let into his apartment after asking Annunciata if he were home. He recognized Thorkild Drehling's voice in an instant, and only now did he recall that Thorkild had mentioned this visit in his card.

He was now clear as to the purpose of this obviously well-planned visit. The whole picture revealed to him—the formal card that might have been written by a diplomat rather than a comrade. The whole choreography of card, atelier, visit. This was a declaration. A leave-taking. As the well-bred son of a property magnate, Thorkild could not just lift his haversack without any further fuss and take off. Oh no... his self-esteem demanded a ceremony. A whole damn pantomime. So be it! A show he would get. He would get a discharge sheet to remember!

When he opened the door to the sitting room, Thorkild had just taken a seat. Ursula sat by the window, gazing out over the city with her chin resting on her hand. Her expression betrayed a dark anxiety. She seemed to have received Thorkild with indifference, almost with cold reluctance.

Jørgen paused at the door. He looked at his friend from this vantage point and gave a forced, ironic smile.

"Aye, aye, shipmate. What a happy coincidence! I have just come from your atelier. May I congratulate you from the heart for your excellent contribution to the new chocolate and confectionary wrapping-paper industry. They are unsurpassed! I've no doubt that they will get bourgeois patisserie hearts pounding like a polka. Get them on the bonbon boxes, man, and you will get a half-sovereign per box!"

Thorkild declined to answer. This was not the kind of tone he wanted while waging this battle. An inevitable clash that had weighed on his mind for so long, and the stage for which he had carefully chosen—here, in Ursula's presence.

"You weren't long in picking up your new expertise, man. Top of the class! ... Sahlmann will be delighted with you. And of course he will be coming down here to join you now that he has got his thirty pieces of silver!" Jørgen warmed to his "schooling," crossing the floor back and forth. Pacing the full length of the sitting room, his struggle to conceal his true animus growing more obvious by the second. "But all this does not surprise me in the least! Quite the opposite! You and Sahlmann are, of course, two fine cuts from the same couture lambskin. As true sons of our blessed little Danish windmill land, you will turn whichever way the wind blows. And that's your lyrical inspiration for you! Ah, don't worry, I know my gallant Danish heroes! ... But really ... warmest congratulations, I do really congratulate you, Drehling! The powers that be like nothing better than a returned prodigal with a dubious past, for which he begs forgiveness. Cap in hand for a few shillings and a humble apology on his lips ... because God knows that's the only way to turn art into a lucrative career these days. So never worry! You too will get your Order of the Garter in the New Year's Honors List. Or if not a garter, a scepter, bauble, or some such great gong!"

Thorkild chose to ignore Jørgen's wounding barbs in his reply.

"Is it really so impossible for you to conceive that people can genuinely change their views on things, and that this might not always be due to cold calculation and self-interest?"

"Calculation? Self-interest? Who mentioned that? That at least would be something! An explanation at least. A bit more like the way real men behave! ... But no ... its's the pathetic, fawning milksop blood that runs in the veins of all you crawlers that I can't stand. The

Mommy's-little-boy-lost still looking for the teat... the cozy cocoon of the bourgeois family. Nice pats on the cheeks at the piano from Auntie and Uncle... the tickle on the tummy you all yearn for, even as grown men. Fie, for shame! In the long run none of you can bear life without Uncle Jeremy and Auntie Maud. That's what I am talking about! This backsliding into the bosom of the wet-nurses that reared all you posh boys!"

"Oh Lord... all this invective about cowardice and hypocrisy has once again become your main hobbyhorse, Jørgen," said Thorkild with a wry smile. "It would never enter your head for a moment that there might be another—far deeper—reason for returning to our shared, age-old artistic ideals, something which, after all, is not just happening in Denmark, but across the whole of Europe, and I thi—"

"Sing it!" Jørgen cried, brutally cutting across him. "I know the whole damn hymn sheet! And Sahlmann is the choirmaster! A new hymn, a new ideal, every week. You change views just like you change a shirt. If one disguise doesn't work, just try a new one. Poets, authors, and artists as court jesters. Charlatans! Circus clowns, who turn themselves inside out to entertain the cultural elite!... Is that the hocus-pocus philosophy that has turned your head? Are these the wonderful age-old artistic ideals you all of a sudden say you worship?"

"Jørgen, if you would just listen for a moment... there is no question of set-in-stone principles or views here. Nothing of the sort. *That* is the whole point. In this new age, when the whole world seems to be standing on a soapbox spouting a set of fixed and unmovable opinions. Surely we are allowed to be open-minded, and yes, have the right *not* to follow any strict dogma or commandments whatsoever. In general, is it not the obligation, and indeed the special preserve, of cultured people to—in all modesty—observe life and existence, develop certain motifs and reflections on those observations, and then—in that inevitably obscure realm—attempt to intuit the dynamic and purpose therein! It is precisely—in my eyes—Sahlmann's great gift, the best proof of his genius, that he, before anyone else in Denmark, renounced all doctrine-posturing and let his own glorious Pegasus graze freely wherever it pleased, instead of the brutish notion of placing a fabled winged steed in harness, like some plodding draft horse, to the social, political, or moral ideas of our time? You cannot pre-plan artistic inspiration, for heaven's sake."

"Ah, now we have it . . . I know your damn sort! Nothing but a pack of unprincipled scoundrels," said Jørgen. He had stopped in the middle of the floor, his arms akimbo, legs and feet planted wide. "The whole catechism of Romanticism, just in a repackaged and newly wrapped edition! Seeing and thinking clearly, and showing things as they are . . . that is once again declared a sign of the highest stupidity! To depict black as black, and white as white . . . that is once again declared to be a lack of intellectual and spiritual discernment! So three cheers for pantomime, smoke and mirrors, and humbug. What is it to you, well-fed dreamers, if millions of your fellow human beings are dying of hunger; that freedom is being trampled into the dust; that the truth is being slowly strangled? Oh no . . . you refined virtuosos are above all that. In your sacred role as keepers of the age-old flame you sit astride your blasted Pegasuses and crest the distant blue mountain peaks, sharing ambrosia with the gods and goddesses. Well met, sir! Hip hip hooray, you chaps! . . . Our age yearns for beauty! Our age yearns for joy! . . . Is not that how those catchphrases go?"

"Yes, exactly!" Thorkild exclaimed.

"Exactly, indeed . . . and you conjurers and magicians are immediately there like adroit head waiters catering to the audience's every whim. A plate of *Joy*, sir?—your humble servant! Master and Mistress require a serving of *Beauty*, do they? . . . No sooner said than done! And the audience is thrilled, and the head waiter gets an Order of the Garter as baksheesh!"

Thorkild recoiled visibly. "Ah, now look here, Hallager—"

But his former comrade gave him no chance to make his point as he once again bestrode the tiled floor with heavier and heavier footfall.

"Of course there is a thirst for beauty in our age! It's the thirst of a drunken sot the day after a spree. We can no longer bear to be sober and clear-eyed. It has gradually become our wont and custom to avoid intellectual sobriety. If we at any point are roused to self-awareness . . .

to a clear understanding of our own wretchedness and that of the world about us ... we become disgusted and terrified and cannot look that corrupted pit in the eye ... the very slime pit in which we choose to wallow. So we desperately seek inebriation once more. Of course! Find blissful amnesia by being in permanent disgrace. And it is to that place—to such a cowardly betrayal of a good and sound life, of the future, yours and mine and all our descendants to come, that you allowed yourself to be tempted and lured astray. You! Yes you, Thorkild Drehling! You of all people in this world!"

Jørgen had once again stopped in the middle of the floor and uttered these last words like a volley of cannon shots. Unnoticed in all this, Ursula, who had been sitting by the window, had stood up and moved to the stove, which was set in a marble fireplace with a mantel ledge. Her arms and upper body were now resting on the mantelpiece. From here, she stared intensely at Jørgen with a countenance that almost spoke of terror.

Thorkild's cheeks had reddened to fire. After a moment to gather himself, he replied very quietly and rather haltingly.

"I admit, I owe you an explanation. But how can I give that explanation if you won't let me speak? What I wanted so say was, well ... well ... it seems to me that you yourself, Jørgen, who are so often found to be agitating against the worship of false gods in our age ... yes ... you yourself have fallen victim to the very malaise you ceaselessly warn against. In other words, Jørgen Hallager has his own false gods. And they are human happiness and the common good in the way that you argue these can be achieved. For example, I believe that you, and also people like me and many others, have overestimated both the burden of poverty and the benefits that so-called freedom will actually deliver for humanity. I will be honest and say that there are times when I even envied a slave in his chains and felt poorer than the wretch who has no roof over his head. It is possible to come from a wealthy background and still suffer!"

"What the hell are you talking about, man? It sounds like you swallowed all this newfangled oracle jargon as well? Don't worry about facts, let hocus-pocus tell us where the problems lie."

"I think I am making my point perfectly clear, Jørgen. What I am saying is . . . that I have . . . learned to believe in a joy for which I would gladly give away the most untrammeled freedom, the treasures of a whole empire, and, yes, even my daily bread. And I now believe . . . in fact I know, that one can suffer sorrows and disappointments in life that gnaw and torture your soul in far more excruciating ways—far far more—than both hunger and cold possibly could."

"And what sorrows might they be, if a man is allowed to ask a straight question?"

"Do you really need to ask? Open your eyes and look around you! . . . Walk down a street, any street, and look at the faces you meet there. For every one marked by hunger or oppression, you will find ten, even twenty, in which you can read like an open book the age-old tale of inner sorrows that have ravaged people since time began, regardless of social rank and class. And yes, in fact, which are possibly felt most strongly by those to whom life has, by the initial looks of it, been most bountiful . . . love worries, worries about parents, feelings of loneliness, sadness, unable to embrace life, unable to face death . . . oh, a million things."

"Absolute rubbish! Unless the things you mention there are the result of some unavoidable misfortune due to a heavy blow from the hand of fate, which mentally strong people always quickly rise above anyway, then it is just more of the same hysterical lamentations by disturbed prima donnas . . . misanthropic and exceptionalist fantasies, for which I have not an ounce of pity. You want to raise the so-called sensitive souls to an elite plane above the rest of the people . . . well, I am sorry; they are flesh and blood like everybody else. No really, Drehling . . . a free and healthy man has no other serious concerns than guarding that freedom and guarding that health. The desire and struggle for freedom and then the drive for self-preservation . . . these are the primordial sentiments of mankind—the spinal cord of the soul and consciousness. These alone are the life and death values that underpin our lives."

"I believe you are grievously wrong in what you say. Life's highest values come from a much deeper and untainted source. That which raises man to great heights, or indeed lays him low, are the great waves of emotion and passion that traverse his soul... our love throes, our longings, our fleeting glimpses of the eternal, our joy when encountering great beauty... the bittersweet melancholy of certain memories, the sense of wonder in what we imagine... in short, the alluring or utterly crushing lyrical strains that dominate human existence. It is for this reason that the lyricism in poetry or painting that you so detest is the pinnacle of art, and in truth, the real purpose and goal of art. It is this supreme poetic aspiration that moved the great masters. For they perceived and felt its power to a far greater degree than most others. That is the reason they acquired their undeniable and indeed immortal significance for mankind."

"There you go again with the ancient past. The glorious past is what we must slavishly imitate! So we all have to spew out the hoary old lyrics of the long-dead bards in yet another generation... the very stinking corpse down in the ship's hold that we are forced to sail with and can never throw overboard!... And, by the devil, we have paid the price for that folly in this new age! Look at the art of our times! In this century, when the human spirit has celebrated triumphs in all fields and endeavors like never before; only the arts have sunk downwards to a despicable pit of spinelessness. And why? Why? Yes—let's look around as you have asked me to do!... In an age of huge upheavals and infernos of rage wherever one looks that are literally earthshaking... in an age when an old millennium is toppling to the grave in thunderous noise and avalanche booms... where are the artists, eh? What great works are our painters, poets, and sculptors engaged in? Go to the exhibitions and galleries and see for yourself, man! Study their catalogues and portfolios! Hell's teeth!... A pretty young girl smelling a rose. An old hag spinning her threads. Moonlight in a garden. A nymph in a forest. What say you?... And the poets and belletrists? Are any of them a single whit better? Read their books! Look at your newfound friend, the great Sahlmann! Love-refrains. Love-laments. Love-waffle—and it is such a degradation of the gift possessed by art, whose calling it is to eulogize and garland the martyrs among our people, and at the same time to curse and flay the tyrants, villains, and dullards... art, which should be the 'lyre and sword' of our new age; the true *vox dei* that imparts and conveys divine justice from generation to generation. It is this art that—ah, stop!... I can barely speak of it anymore! It's too base and rotten, too cowardly, too outrageous—no, no!"

Jørgen Hallager could no longer speak, so great was his vehemence. The words stayed lodged in his throat. All he could do was make a violent waving movement with his arm to dismiss even the thought of contradiction. He then moved to the window and simply stood there looking out—struggling with his inner turmoil.

For several minutes, a deathly silence reigned in the room. Through the open balcony windows, birds could be heard cooing on the roof, and from the square below came the cries and shouts of street hawkers.

Then Thorkild stood up.

"I don't see much point in trying to continue this conversation," he said.

"Neither do I," Jørgen replied.

Silence once again.

"Well then... I can only bid you farewell?"

"Goodbye," said Jørgen, without turning around.

Still Thorkild hesitated. But when Jørgen made no sign that he would turn to face him, he moved towards Ursula. She was still standing at the mantelpiece. Her head was buried in her hands.

"Farewell, Fru Hallager!"

But Ursula too declined to look at him, or even to place her hand in his outstretched palm. She merely answered his greeting with an almost imperceptible movement of her now bleach-white lips.

With this, he fully understood that Ursula Branth was once more in Jørgen's dominion. Thus, with his head bowed, he quietly left the room. From within, the occupants of the room could not fail to notice how he closed the hall door behind him with barely a sound; in the manner of someone leaving a sickbed or a wake-house.

Jørgen turned from the window and walked back and forth in the sitting room a few times, muttering to himself. Then he sat down in the armchair with his hands in front of his face.

Throughout the whole violent exchange—a thing unknown to her between friends—Ursula had not moved an inch. And for another while, she remained standing motionless, completely gripped by her own turmoil. Finally, she raised her head and with slow, tottering steps, went to Jørgen, steadied herself, and without a sound placed her hand on his shoulder.

He gave a start and looked up. He had almost forgotten her presence.

"What? What is it?" he asked in a curt tone.

"Jørgen ... we have to talk about things!"

"What do you mean?"

She hesitated.

"Will you explain, Jørgen ... really explain this time ... how it is you became ... the way you are?"

"What do you mean? ... We are born the way we are born, as you know. Some enter the world straight-backed and others humpbacked. In our days mostly the latter."

They both fell to silence.

"Jørgen," said Ursula, still standing with her hand on his shoulder and gazing at the floor. "Tell me something about you. I mean you as a person. It's been so long since you did."

"What do you want me to tell?"

"Tell me how ... I mean *when* did you get the opinions and thoughts you have now. Because you can't always have had those views, surely?"

"Very strange that you are suddenly showing such a great interest in me and my opinions. Lately you have been quick enough to interrupt me as soon as I begin stating them! ... And anyway, I have already told you about my childhood and my upbringing. That's explanation enough, I think."

"Yes, yes. That's true. But tell me, Jørgen ... was there a single moment ... I mean a particular moment? A moment you can identify, and say *that* was when the life view I have now was formed ... from that moment on?"

He did not answer right away.

"A particular moment?" he said finally, lost in his own thoughts. "Oh, yes, I suppose there was, all right."

"Oh, do tell me. Tell me all about it," Ursula begged, as if roused from a trance. She pulled a stool over and sat at his feet. "Look, I'm sitting here now! I'm not going to let you push me away. You will be good and kindly with me... and tell me what happened."

By now Jørgen had fully turned to look at her properly.

"Good grief, Ursula!... You are white as a sheet. And a bit too overwrought for my liking. I think you should lie down for a while."

"No, Jørgen, really... I am in top form. When I am with you, just me and you... and when I hear you speaking softly... I just love it. And I'm not overwrought at all, Jørgen. Look, here's little Ursula at your feet. I'm quite calm, honestly. But I need, need, need you very much. And I know you are going to teach me, bear me up, school me in our new life together... aren't you, darling?"

Jørgen had once again sunk back into his dark reflections.

"A particular moment?" he said again. "Did I never tell you about the day when my father was arrested by the police in the middle of teaching a class?"

"No, Jørgen, you never did... Tell me, love. Tell me everything!"

He balked for a while longer. He was bent forward, almost double, with his elbows propped on his knees, both fists under his chin, and staring at some space in the distance.

"It's a long time ago now. I was fourteen years old then and was getting ready for confirmation... all the rituals of Bible study and confession, of course. This was my father's first post as a fully fledged teacher. Before that he had only been an assistant teacher, helping an old deacon in East Jutland, where he had always been at odds with the parish priest and the other leading lights of the district. The old priest was a pig of a man, and he was a lecher to boot... He had several affairs going at the same time with different farmers' wives. The district doctor claimed a fortune in fees from the Parish Relief Fund for medicines the poor neither saw nor were even recommended in the first place. As for the local magistrate... well, if he got a few pounds of butter or a few fat ducks under the table, he didn't mind turning a blind eye to all the strokes these hypocrites were pulling. Now, my father was never a man that could see all this happening and not protest, never mind whether it was himself or others who were the victims. So it happened that the old deacon died one day and, instead of giving him the expected promotion to the teaching post proper, these scoundrels got Father shifted to a poorly paid backwater teaching post right over on the harshest of coasts in West Jutland, in Ringkøbing, and he never saw his home district again. But those utter dogs still had a rod for his back, even though they were rid of him! You see . . . as assistant teacher, father was obliged to act as administrator for the Parish Health Board and they now complained to the police that they had discovered he had embezzled the funds. Right in the middle of teaching a class, my father was arrested, and as he protested and refused to accompany the officers voluntarily, they clapped handcuffs on him right in front of the schoolchildren and dragged him off."

"And was your father indeed completely innocent?"

"Father would have bitten off all his fingers rather than cheat another human being of a single penny. It was precisely that mirror of strict morality he held up to those blackguards that spurred their hatred of him. It broke their chain of corrupt custom and practice. And so he was pronounced a 'rebel.' My mother just assumed the whole thing was due to some huge misunderstanding and expected his return home the very same day. But instead the police came again—a three-man search team—and turned our home upside down. Every single object and space in our home was ransacked. Every note and scrap of paper father had ever written on. Even the personal letters from my mother and father's engagement period were taken out and read, one by one, and openly mocked. Not even my mother's physical person was spared. When they were finally done with this act of shame, one of these curs threw a gross insult at Mother, quoting from their private letters and saying she would not have her bosom man to cling to in her bed for a year or more. And then they left. Mother collapsed with the shock . . . she had never had a strong constitution and she never recovered from it. That night, while I was lying awake and hearing Mother sob, I swore a solemn and binding oath to myself... which I think I have kept."

"And did all that happen exactly as you have described it, Jørgen?"

"As I have said!... But that's not all! Father was suspended from office, as it is officially called. And as he had creditors, his estate was declared bankrupt. The powers that be were so kind as to grant us a grace period, and some of the local people offered us help, but I told mother not to accept a single handout. I was the man of the house now. Never would they get the extra satisfaction of seeing us beg! For weeks, we lived off little more than stale bread and potato peelings that I scraped out of pigswill barrels. I should have been confirmed that Easter but was turned away by the priest because I had given a lad who called my father a common thief a thrashing. Some time after that, I got an apprentice position with a master painter in a neighboring town and mother began to do sewing work for folk... and so we eked out an existence through the summer."

"But your father? They apologized on bended knee in the end? He received compensation and was exonerated?"

"An apology? Bended knee? Not at all... Of course they had to acquit him in the end. Officially, due to lack of evidence. But he was in custody for half a year, and the brand mark of thief stuck with him for the rest of his life. And then when Mother died and he was left alone, he sought consolation where many others have before him. I do not blame him for that! And I did so even less when I was younger. Naturally enough, I saw in his life a unique and extraordinary martyrdom. But with age and experience I know that the opposite is the case! I soon learned that my father's fate is what awaits all free and upstanding men among us. One must bend the knee before the tyrant and suffer his villainy in silence—otherwise you are thrown into the pit like a diseased animal!"

He lapsed into silence.

Ursula remained sitting on the low stool. Her hands folded in her lap. She sat there staring. Her large, dark eyes looking outwards but seeming to see nothing. The stare of a sleepwalker.

"Jørgen," she said. She was barely audible. "I believe . . . I am there. With you."

"Yes, that's what you said earlier today. Tomorrow, when you are in different form, you will forget the promise you have just made."

"No, no, I swear." She lifted one hand and stroked her forehead slowly. "It is as if I have been roused from a long, long sleep. I see everything so clearly. I now understand everything . . . including myself. Yes, for now I know it . . . yes, I have thought these thoughts and felt all these things before. They just didn't enter my heart until now. You have gifted me that! . . . Yes, that's how it is! Many times at home, when I lay in my bed in the evening, and I heard the storm howling, and the fire shone in my tiled stove . . . and when I then thought of those people who were abroad on such a night, no roof over their heads and not even a crust of bread to eat . . . I could suddenly freeze in my warm bed till my skin cracked . . . I felt like a thief who had stolen the last penny from a poor man's purse . . . yes, I wished God would punish me! That I myself would be made poor and wretched, forced to walk around with bare feet in the snow and sing at the doors to beg for that dry bread!"

Jørgen looked down at her. It was a look of dark, hopeless resignation. All at once she rose, and stood for a while quite motionless with her hands pressed flat against her eyes.

"Ursula," Jørgen warned.

But she did not hear him. She tore her hands from her face, grabbed a gold chain she wore around her neck, and flung it to the floor.

"Don't touch it! Let it lie there forever now! Away with all finery and damn fallalery now! A worm have I been! A tramp have I been."

"Ursula!" roared Jørgen, a threat in his voice now as he sprang to his feet.

"Yes, my love . . . I'm coming! I'm coming!" She was almost exultant now and first loosened then threw away the tortoiseshell comb from her hair, so that it fell in dark, cascading waves around her white dress. Then she spread her arms and stared at him with large, radiant eyes. "Yes, here I am! Here I am at last! . . . Now I am completely yours! Free, strong, and happy! Striving upwards. Ever upwards. Come,

come—my dear friend. My beloved! Now our life can truly begin! Now can we march side by side! ... From door to door will we go ... with the poor, and with those who suffer distress ... hand in hand, you and I my love ... come! And we will."

Jørgen could no longer contain himself.

"Shut your damn mouth!" he bellowed with all his force and raised his fist at her.

At this Zeus-like thunderclap in the room, a violent jolt went through Ursula. She stared at him for a moment as if turned to stone. Then she placed her hands to either side of her head in a silent scream. Her cheeks changed color, her eyes closed, and with a strangled sigh she sank to the floor.

Jørgen lifted her into his arms and carried her to the bedroom. He assumed it was yet another of the sudden fainting spells she had been suffering of late and splashed water on her face. But when she did not come around or even respond, and when he felt slight but peculiar convulsions rippling through her body, he became seriously alarmed. He ran out to the kitchen and roared:

"Annunciata! Annunciata! The doctor. The doctor! *Medico! Medico!* Hurry!"

In the early evening, State Councilor Branth rounded the street corner into Via della Purificazione. His purpose was to pay his daughter a visit, but he lingered, as he now always did, outside the apartment building, walking the pavement back and forth a couple of times while summoning the courage to go up there. Then he finally slipped in through the outer entrance gate and, with increasing shortness of breath, slowly ascended the steep staircase. When he finally reached the fifth floor, he was surprised to find the apartment door wide open, and on entering he found little Annunciata sitting crouched in a corner. She was clearly distressed and in floods of tears.

"What on earth is wrong here?" the state councilor asked with trepidation.

The child threw her arms out in a wild gesture and whimpered:

"*Mia signora! ... Mia signora!*"

At the same moment, the bedroom door opened and a gentleman

stepped out. It was not Jørgen Hallager. It was a Danish doctor resident in Rome, whom State Councilor Branth knew very well.

"What has happened to my daughter?" he asked, his body already trembling like a leaf.

The doctor's answer was evasive. He asked Hr. Branth to be seated, to compose himself and prepare for grave news. He spoke of a seizure, and bleeding in the brain...

"I want to see her! I want to see my child!" the old man shouted, and before the doctor could stop him, he rushed into the bedroom.

Inside, the windows and external shutters were closed; the room was extremely dark, but for a sole candle burning at the bedside table. Hr. Branth saw the janitress fussing with a cleaning cloth at the headrest of the large, canopied and curtained four-poster bed. The flickering amber glow from the candle flitted intermittently across the bed, where Ursula lay on her back—stiff and motionless, her face starch-white, and the eyes nothing more than dim hollows.

"Dead! My child is dead!" he screamed, as he threw himself onto the bed, from whence he emitted a heartrending whine.

Speaking in Italian, which the state councilor understood quite well, the janitress blessed herself and sought to console him. "Yes, Signore, the good lady has suffered her last. Let that be of comfort to you. We will all pray for the good lady. And be sure Our Holy Mother will intercede for her and help raise her up. Very soon she will be happily placed in the arms of the eternal God. She called out to the Lord many times in her last moments! 'Father, Father, Father!' she kept calling. Oh don't worry, I understood her words! It was Our Lord in heaven she called upon. We sent messengers for you, sir, but you were not at home, and that is very sad. Because you didn't see her before she died. Ah, dear dear... She was a lovely, lovely, kind lady!"

The old man rose with great difficulty from the bed and looked about the room. There in its darkest corner his gaze met Jørgen Hallager's, who was sitting bent over with his face in his hands.

"Murderer! Murderer!... Murderer! You have murdered my only child!" he shouted, and rushed with raised arms towards him. But the doctor who had followed him into the room now intervened and gripped his arm with no little force.

"State Councilor Branth will compose himself this instant," he said in a commanding tone.

Jørgen Hallager had not moved a muscle. His whole facility for thought had seized up. He understood none of it. He was dumbfounded and shocked to his core. The whole thing seemed like some riddle he was unable to fathom.

8

A FEW YEARS had passed by.

In Denmark, the long struggle for a new democratic constitution staggered to a final, if muddled, resolution. True, the warring parties still retained a notional threat of armed action, be that state authorized or from the radical side. The right wing still wished to give the reigning monarch a role in appointing government and the retention of aristocratic influence in the upper parliamentary chamber, while the left wing sought to make the lower chamber of parliament the sole arbiter. The much smaller revolutionary groups sought a complete removal of the aristocracy and monarchy from political life. However, the two biggest factions on either side—weary of the unending friction—now looked to smooth out the major differences and come to a point of compromise. In particular, the previously left-wing People's Party, which had been at the center of demands for constitutional change, showed an ever-increasing tendency to reconciliation. It was now regarded by all observers as merely a question of time, or face-saving etiquette, as to when their final acceptance of the compromise—or surrender, as the more radical elements viewed it—would take place.

It was at just this political juncture, that the veteran royal couple celebrated their golden wedding anniversary, and the populace seized this pretext to put aside all previous disputes in order to salute Their Majesties in the requisite fashion. From all parts of the country, and from every stratum of society, deputations and emissaries gathered as an endless train of royal subjects presenting a guard of honor before the royal throne. In other words, what had started off as a private family celebration grew quite organically into an event of historical significance and effectively provided an hors d'oeuvre for the reconciliation-fest that was the real catalyst for this national outpouring and the thing for which everyone yearned.

The royal festivities lasted for several days and saw a huge influx of spectators from every other country in Europe. For almost a week, Copenhagen—as the capital of Denmark—basked in the status of a major world city in terms of rank and reputation. And it has to be said that she was well able to carry her newfound celebrity in these blooming days of May. For this was a city of splendor. A fairy-tale city, adorned with flowers and flags. And the good Lord himself provided wondrous sunshine to bless the festivities, and yet the odd peal of thunder in the far distance as its own twenty-one-gun salute to proceedings. Folk festivals and marching columns with rows of fluttering standards alternated with an array of illuminations and fireworks. And wherever the tall, straight-backed royal couple appeared, bestowing waves, smiles, greetings, and clear joy on all sides, and often accompanied by a resplendent retinue of princely kith and kin, the air resounded to the echo with cheers, and many eyes glistened with tears. Among the most popular regal visitors were the king and queen of Greece, English and Russian princesses, but first and foremost the royal couple's son-in-law, the White Czar himself, who was the sole ruler of all Russia and its peoples. In these extraordinary days, a sense of community and patriotism, an enthusiastic belief in the future, reminiscent of the great times of war victories or deep tribulations in the country was reborn. Even the most dejected soul could not help but be swept along by the public fervor. Even the originally indifferent, yes downright oppositional and hostile, to all these celebrations were carried away by the verve and spectacle of it all. After such a long time of strife and sackcloth and ashes, there was a widespread sense of common purpose, of brotherhood, of a solid, unified people, of a nation.

Though not entirely everybody. Late one evening, a closed confederacy sat at a table overflowing with slops and empty beer bottles. The confederates were sitting in a dingy cellar café located in a poorly lit backstreet. Far away from the raucous noise produced by the festivities, the floral displays, the street and shop-front illuminations. Chief among this group was Jørgen Hallager. Sitting with him was the young satirical cartoonist Theobald. Also present was the drink-sodden journalist Hans Braage; a positively ugly, beanpole-thin bookbinder by the name of Reinald was also there, as well as a few other workers or tradesman-types. The company was further embellished by three or four ladies whose purpose could not be mistaken.

This assemblage was in fact the sorry remnants of the once potent Dregs group. Or "the Rearguard," as it now described itself. Its small cadre clique was increased slightly by a few members of a small sect with the grand title of the Revolutionary Workers' Party, who had attached themselves to "the Rearguard" in the hope of recruiting some members.

It was in this grimy, seldom-visited boozing den that these confederates had their usual meeting place; especially at this time, when they would gather every evening to discuss events and topics thrown up by the festivities. At this moment, the drink-sodden journalist was sitting with a small shag pipe under his pocked, bulbous red nose, reading aloud from newspaper articles about the festival in the establishment press. But tonight there was no real conviction in the mocking laughter that occasionally interrupted these reports. Even the best jokes fell flat. The spontaneous joy out in the city that day had been overwhelming and was undeniable. Even well-known left-wing orators had taken part in the festival parade and the viewing of the illuminations.

Jørgen Hallager sat mute and listless in his chair. Emptying his beer glass seeming to be his only interest. His red hair and beard were now as wild-grown and unkempt as in his pre-marriage days. Overall he looked quite foundered. The new times had not been to his favor in any respect. Just recently, his large painting of striking workers had been rejected by the Spring Exhibition. Worse still, this rejection was barely commented upon, not even in the art world, never mind among the general public. Hallager's whole output and the artistic tendency he espoused were now regarded as old hat and hackneyed.

The large audience, which had previously taken such an avid interest in Red Jørgen precisely because he offended and outraged them, had gradually grown indifferent to him and his paintings, which anyway were quite repetitious in subject matter and style. By stark contrast, several of his former comrades and disciples had won widespread acclaim in recent years; first and foremost among these was Thorkild Drehling. His *Merman* painting being one such example. The powerful image of this titan of the sea, oblivious to the ferocious waves, and sending his poignant, searching gaze across the wild coastline and dunes had been received with unbridled praise. Art connoisseurs and critics, meanwhile, especially in the conservative press—which had already long proclaimed the rebirth of Romanticism in literature and art—greeted this still young artist with a fervor that bordered on hysteria. But of course this exaggerated zeal was bound up with their satisfaction at seeing a social realist from the Dregs group becoming a convert to age-old classicalism. However, this "Agnete and the Merman" painting was only a prelude to an even greater success. For that very spring, Drehling had provoked an even greater sensation in the arts world with his vision of the Piramide Cestia—the site of the Protestant cemetery, with its ancient pyramid of Cestius, in Rome—the place where Ursula Branth's remains were interred. Drehling's evocative presentation of the tall, somber cypress trees juxtaposed with the striking white marble, sang of the profound peace that reigns among the hallowed dead and the graves that commemorate them. Sang most of all of a proud, solitary, and homeless soul's longing for eternal peace and rest.

The broad, hefty woman with the red-blotched skin who was sitting next to Jørgen, her arms propped at her sides in the manner of a wrestler, was a now rekindled former flame—a seamstress called Nalle from the rough-and-ready Saxogade area of Copenhagen. The name, or nickname, Nalle being generally avoided as a forename by respectable society, due to its connotations with a bang, a blow, or highly lewd behavior. Be that as it may, this Nalle was in fact the very same lass whom Hallager had described as his gorgeous bit of skirt in those bygone days when he and Thorkild Drehling were still "comrades." His offhand remarks to Drehling that he might marry her now made a reality. Nalle did nothing the whole time but sit and yawn widely, thus revealing her two rows of worm-eaten tooth stubs. And when the drone of the journalist's interminable reading aloud became more and more sleep-inducing, and not least when some of the company had actually fallen asleep, she finally cleared her throat loudly, dug in Hallager's side with her elbow, and motioned with her thumb. He nodded in agreement, emptied his final glass, and got up. The others immediately followed where he led. The hour was also very late by now. The landlord was obliged to let them out by a back door in deference to the police's strict ban on late-night drinking.

Moments afterwards, they were all standing in the street and took leave of each other with their old watchword: "Keep the gunpowder dry, comrade!"

Jørgen and his wife lived on the far side of the Vesterbro area and had a good walk ahead of them. Thus, arm in arm, they drifted through a series of dark backstreets until they reached the flag- and flower-bedecked main thoroughfares. All was quiet and still; people having retired early to gather strength for the excitement and exertions of the next festival day to come. Only at the town-hall square did they meet a pair of lovers, who were standing in the middle of the square, looking with interest at a strange cloud formation, which like a dark, ponderous animal was traversing the kind of bright summer night sky that is peculiar to Scandinavia. The young man was highly animated and seemed to be pointing at something up above and explaining, while the young woman with the pale face and dark flowing hair leaned her cheek against his shoulder and offered an upturned look of love that sent a lance through Jørgen's heart. A shiver in the night cold. That was precisely how Ursula used to stand when she looked at something beautiful or magical . . . Ursula, who now slept the eternal sleep down there between the tall, dark, somber cypress trees. Beneath the long rows of white marble . . . Ah, pure bilgewater, Hallager! . . . That woman who two years ago was buried in a cemetery in Rome and now rotted in a coffin that cost an arm and a leg.

His wife roused him from his reveries by saying: "I don't care what you say, Jørgen . . . but that there uz right pretty and nice all the same."

"Eh? What are you on about?"

"All these many flags and decorations and greenery everywhere. It's like poetry . . . or like in a theater only you don't have to pay."

"Good grief, Nalle . . . I think, by all the gods, you are getting a bad dose of lyricism. It'll be the meaning of existence next!"

"Lyricism? Now what are *you* on about, dear man?"

"Lyricism? Do you not know that, my lass! . . . Damn, where do I start? You see . . . it's the mystical smoke and incense that's needed before you can see and appreciate beauty! You catch it off a weak constitution and bad digestion. A lyricist is nothing but a man with a bad stomach."

"You are never done mocking me, Jørgen. For that is nothing but a tall tale, I know."

"Do you think so? . . . Well, you may make a good note of it anyway, my girl. Because at the end of the day, this is where the whole tragedy starts and ends. For there is no point in denying it . . . the idealists are actually right, and we socialists, anarchists, and nihilists are a bunch of dunderheads. Oh yes . . . I see it more and more clearly every day! Freedom? Ha! It's not freedom that can save us. Not society that is wrong. It is ourselves . . . Lyricism has entered the human psyche. And that's like getting mold and damp throughout a building. Children will never grow strong and thrive there, as you know! No great future lies in wait there. And there is no point trying to patch it up here and there. The whole shebang has to be ripped down to the ground. Not a shred of the old mold must remain . . . there is no other salvation! Of course, history has shown an example of this before.—Are you still with me, Nalle? It is neither new laws we need, nor new thinking on justice . . . nor is it new continents that can give us fresh impetus—that idea is all the rage at the moment by the way. Well, if it's a new America we need, it's not the one on the map but a new America in man himself! Do you get my point? . . . A pure and uncultivated spot within each of us. Virginal! With no past. No recollections. No damn Renaissance around our necks. Or any other remnants in dark nooks and crannies where the rot and mold can worm its way in, gain nourishment and spread its canker. Do you understand?"

Red Jørgen continued to develop and proclaim these ideas at length, while his wife demonstrated her engagement by an incessant stream of loud yawns.

At last they arrived home.

They lived in an area populated by manual workers and their families—the Matthaeus quarter. Theirs was a two-room loft dwelling in which one room served as both a living room and Jørgen Hallager's "atelier." Once inside, they were received by a small poisonous-looking woman. She was sickly green of hue and sported a filthy patch over one eye . . . this was their neighbor, Madam Hansen, who had reluctantly agreed to mind their now three-month-old son in the absence of the mother.

"Back again, Madam Hansen!" Jørgen cried, positively beaming as he immediately went to the cot to look at his child. "How's my brave little recruit been?"

"How's he been? she snarled. "Lor . . . how's the little cratur supposed to be? With his own mother out gallivanting late into the night worse than a common street hussy? He has just fallen asleep there now. Before that he lay there rawling and caterwauling. As if he was being bled! The little rogue. He has me destroyed, I swear!"

"Bravo!" cried Jørgen. "It does a man a power of good to hear that there's at least someone with a bit of bile in them! . . . And you shouldn't take too much offense at the child's roaring, Madam Hansen! My Niels Peter is a chip off the old block. He's already a dyed-in-the-wool street urchin . . . he's just strengthening his bellows, madam! The last thing he wants to be is a confounded lyricist, let me tell you, my good lady!"

"A body would nearly think you had studied for the priesthood, Hr. Hallager . . . the many daft, nonsensical words you can come out with," Madame Hansen fired back at him, as she retreated into the kitchen, where Nalle had begun bustling about with cups and the coffee pot.

Jørgen sat down by the cot and began to look at the tiny pale baby.

A lamp devoid of a glass globe burned on the table, throwing a stark flickering gleam around the white walls of the room, which were covered with paintings. These were either sketches and studies, or fully realized artworks. One would look in vain for anything that accommodated the latest tastes in art. The ever-growing urge among the younger artists to romanticize and look for the exalted had, in Jørgen Hallager, merely provoked a redoubled passion for unapologetic veracity; an even stricter drive in him to depict real human life, real natural existence ... he was—to use the patronizing moniker for him that was used by his fellow artists—"the Last of the Mohicans."

Hallager himself was fully aware of the hopelessness of his position. With a grim and melancholic sense of resignation, he constantly told himself that he could do no other than, with steadfastness and patience, remain at the rearguard post at which fate had placed him in this gloomy, cloying, endless age of darkness that had descended on humanity with its foul, reeking vapors. He was, therefore, doubly glad that his wife Nalle had given him his little Niels Peter, who might one day become his replacement when he grew too old or drink-ridden ... just as he himself had taken over the post of defender of the sacred flame of truth from his father before him. Niels Peter would hopefully, in turn, beget *his* replacement in the form of another little recruit, and that one again a new one, and so on and so on until a bright new dawn did finally rise.

Madam Hansen came in again from the kitchen, bound a tattered shawl around her tight, withered shoulders and head and bade him good night.

"Good night, Madam Hansen," Jørgen called to her, lifting his massive head from its thoughts. "And thank you for being so kind as to mind the new recruit."

"Ah, you with your recruit!" she muttered to herself. "If I may say, Hr. Hallager ... what way is that to rear a child with such an unchristian name. Can you not just stick with his actual name ... Niels Peter? You should be ashamed of yourself, sir."

"Ach, Madam Hansen! I think you might grasp it better than you think. You are such a no-nonsense, sensible woman ... really ... I mean it. Incapable of flattery, madam! One of my people! If I had not gone mooching around Nalle again, I might have wanted to marry your very self! For Nalle is a bit of a dreamer, truth be told. But not you, madam! Am I right?...There's not a trace of lyricism in your whole being. Why...I could kiss you! Truly, Madam Hansen, you are one of the chosen few, whom the Lord has saved from the new Great Flood that will wash away all sin and renew humanity in the generations to come."

"I've never heard such poppycock in all my years, Hr. Hallager. Are you quite right in the head?"

"Poppycock, Madam Hansen? Now, don't start getting all fine with me! Why do you not stick with your own speech and strike me dead with rubbish, drivel, and dung? Do you not understand what I mean, madam? Perhaps those damn dreamers and idealists were right after all! I recall what a stuck-up lawyer once said...He said we had worried so much about bodily health, we had failed in our duty to look after the spirit. That's why, says he, there was so much sadness in the world and so little joy. The fat pig was right!...Has it never struck you, Madam Hansen, how disjointed things have turned out in this world of ours? We have learned to pull all the teeth from people's gobs and put in new ones. Rip open the stomachs of our fellow man and scrub the infected guts till they shine again and life can be good once more. We have invented plasters, pills, and ointments for every disease under the sun...but now...our terminal soul-infection, which eats away at every man...nobody has yet come up with a hot-bath treatment for that! Or what's your view of getting bled, Madam Hansen? I mean a proper powerful one with leeches instead of a barber's bowl? You are a woman of the people, my good lady, who still believes in bloodletting. Am I right?...And yet you can't fathom why I call Niels Peter my little 'recruit'? Have you not noticed that blessed street-thief face he has on him already? Just wait, madam! That lad will go far! Especially with the right upbringing. He will be his own Land of the Free. A walking New America!... Do you not think so, Madam Hansen?"

Madam Hansen, who had stood looking at him with a mixture

of pity and indignation, did not deign to give an answer. It was a well-known fact that Hr. Hallager was stone-mad.

"Hmph! Good night to you, sir," she snorted as she turned to the door.

"Good night, Madam Hansen! . . . And keep your bile boiling!"

TRANSLATOR'S NOTE

On Thorkild Drehling's "Merman" Painting

WITH ITS extremely extensive coastline regions and sophisticated maritime culture, Scandinavia is unsurprisingly a fount of nautical legends. Even before the Viking age, seafaring was highly developed and central to the dynamic that launched large numbers of Scandinavians on a never-to-return odyssey west and southwards, as part of what became known as the Migration Period. In its time, the seamanship and river navigation of the Vikings in the following epoch was as groundbreaking as the space travel of our own era. The Vikings could literally go anywhere.

Out of this maritime culture came many sea stories that explored the idea of human interaction with sea gods and sea creatures. Probably the most famous is Hans Christian Andersen's gruesome "The Little Mermaid" ("Den lille Havfrue"). The love-besotted Mermaid achieves her wish of obtaining human form but, as the witch who facilitated this existential change warned her, every step on her new human legs would be as blades going through her body. "The Little Mermaid" has many similarities with the Merman story that is so important to Henrik Pontoppidan's *The Rearguard*. The Merman legend is famous as "Agnete og Havmanden" ("Agnes and the Merman") in Denmark. We do not need much encouragement to perceive that Ursula Branth is Agnes and Jørgen Hallager the ferocious Merman.

The most popular version of the Merman tale relates that Agnes is carried off from the wild windswept coast where she lives to the Merman's underwater dwelling. In the briny depths, she bears him seven sons. But Agnes hears the church bells of her birthplace and longs to go above. To attend church among her own kind. The Merman agrees but sets conditions: that she keep her hair tied when in the vicinity of the church, not allowing it to float free; that she does not sit with her mother in church; and that she does not genuflect at the mention of the holy name in the service. Having consented to these terms, Agnes betrays the Merman and never returns. She cleaves to her natural essence and reenters the fold of "civilized" humanity.

"Agnete og Havmanden" was published as a fly-bill, or flying sheet, for gatherings and taverns in the eighteenth century and further explored by poets and playwrights like the influential Jens Baggesen. In 1843, Andersen staged his own version of "Agnes and the Merman," though it proved a fiasco. For Pontoppidan, Kierkegaard's extended study of the Merman myth in one of his greatest books, *Fear and Trembling* (1843), was even more important than the other sources. He appears to have read the book in 1894. In *Fear and Trembling*, Kierkegaard's Johannes de Silentio draws the previous versions of the story together in a set of different scenarios and examines the ethical and existential choices that were open to both Agnes and the Merman. Crucially for our purposes Agnes (Ursula) can be drawn to the Wildman as is described in the legend. In the lovemaking scene at the start of events (which would have been considered quite racy in Pontoppidan's day), Ursula describes Hallager as her "great, big barbarian wild man." But the Merman can be so overpowered by Agnes's innocence and trust in him that he cannot bring himself to carry her off. (Hallager simply crushes Ursula's innocence.) Or alternatively the Merman retreats from Agnes due to his love for her and enters a realm of silence. Appropriately, he attains Kierkegaard's heightened "demonic" state by declining supplication to the miracle of forgiveness but lets Agnes go. (Hallager keeps hold of Ursula to the bitter end.) Or finally, via a miracle and leap of faith, the Merman can become fully human, repent his former life, and confess his past to his beloved, at which point Agnes will forgive him. She is Agnus Dei who forgives the sins of the world. (The idea of apologizing would never occur to Hallager.)

In the folk legend, the Merman always remains a denizen of the deep and never undergoes an existential change. But his Mermaid does. First, she transforms into a sea creature but eventually resumes her human shape. Thorkild Drehling's painting does not tell the whole story of the Merman and Agnes. He shows the Merman beast waiting by the sea rocks in the forlorn hope that his mate will return. Drehling's clear message to Ursula with this painting is that she should return to civilization. Preferably not only by embracing the painting but also by embracing him. The painting demonstrates his newfound values as an artist but its overly subtle message reveals a lack of self belief and true conviction in love. In this life-and-death situation, readers feel subtle hints are shown for what they are—pathetic. What Ursula urgently needs is a dauntless champion who will risk all to save his love. Instead, Drehling quietly slips away. Indeed, Drehling's milksop approach to life is precisely what Hallager ridicules him for. We can almost feel Pontoppidan's exasperation with Drehling.

None of the three main characters in *The Rearguard* can make an existential leap beyond themselves. Pontoppidan's general literary thrust is that this is typical of modern Danes. They are unable to break out of the life roles for which heredity and upbringing have prepared them. And it can be argued that Hallager represents an even more pronounced state of that rigidity—that inability to change—because his blind adherence to an ideological position and rejection of the idea of all-conquering love, and therefore care of the "other," succeeds in nothing but dragging people down to destruction and driving away his companions and comrades.

In this remarkable short novel, which manages to meld revolutionary politics with art and myth, Hallager may despise Drehling's painting as hocus-pocus, but he is himself, readers quickly sense, all too like the Merman, just as Ursula, drawn to him, resembles the Merwoman. And yet, true to his artistic form, Pontoppidan complicates the relationship between his characters and those of the Merman tale. So while Hallager is indeed portrayed as a brute, his laceration of conservative hypocrites is given its due regard. Pontoppidan provides a compelling justification for Hallager's aggressiveness, given the horrendous events of his childhood and bourgeois society's witch hunt against his father with the effect that Hallager emerges as a uniquely complicated figure, a challenge to the moral imagination of readers.

Pontoppidan's approach to fiction is polyphonic. He employs a dialectical irony that Georg Lukács described as a new literary development. Pontoppidan drives his characters to confront the issue of their true selves and how they should live their lives. Some invisible force seems ever to force them to a point of crisis, even at the height of success. Nor do his readers escape unchallenged. Given that all the characters and scenarios are ironized, there is no authorial guide as to what we should think. Readers are forced to reflect on those characters, their statements and actions, and make a decision, as to not just what they themselves think but also what they would do in this situation. How they should live their lives, in other words.

In the early part of his literary career, Pontoppidan's work was heavily social realist in style and expressed a clear anger at living conditions for the common man and woman. An anger that sometimes reaches Hallager dimensions and portrays society's iniquities in the graphic style of a Hallager painting, with no attempt at literary flourishes and demonstrative lyricism. This style, Pontoppidan once said, was a parvenu form of art. However, with *The Rearguard*—first serialized in the 1890s—we see a marked shift to a more expansive set of themes, which though still encompassing anticlericalism, social anger, and politics, also embraces a more profound look at sexual relations and a much deeper exploration of philosophical life-views. *The Rearguard* marks a decisive move in this direction. A move to the polyphonic.

In the voice and character of Hallager, Pontoppidan provides an eerily prophetic vision of the demagoguery the world would witness with the Stalinist perversion of socialism in the twentieth century. Perhaps only Herman Melville's Ahab offers a comparable vision of obsessive monomania and the dangers it presents to people and society. And yet—and there is always a "yet," always the other side of the argument with Pontoppidan—Hallager's harrowing tale of the injustices heaped upon his father and mother, as well as the blatant hypocrisy of those eminent members of society who meted out that injustice, means that *The Rearguard* also poses hard questions for civic society. Why and how, we must ask, does such stubborn ferocity arise in the first place?

The Rearguard and its characters highlight one of the challenges facing Pontoppidan's reception, which has increased apace in modern times. And that is that readers and critics alike want glib, off-pat statements from Pontoppidan—we might call them clickable memes these days—about his own life-view and how his works should be read. He refuses to do this. There is no road map. Readers are compelled to read his works deeply and work out their own life-view. In this he follows Nietzsche and Kierkegaard, but far more than either of these "self-torturers"—as he was wont to ironize both of them—looms the figure of Socrates. If that master of irony Pontoppidan had a constant life-mantra it was after Socrates's "know thyself."

It is in Socrates's embracing of life in all its facets, his happy confidence, his bravery in sticking to his own position but encouraging others not to follow him but to work out their own life-view that we must see Pontoppidan's portrayal of the ingrained bully Hallager and the dithering flower Drehling. Where Ursula is concerned, in the shocking finale of *The Rearguard*, Pontoppidan seems to insist that she should have stood on her own two philosophical feet and then reached for her own stars, rather than slavishly hitching her fate to the blazing Hallager comet as it hurtled to its inevitable doom.

—Paul Larkin

OTHER NEW YORK REVIEW CLASSICS

For a complete list of titles, visit www.nyrb.com.

OĞUZ ATAY Waiting for the Fear
HONORÉ DE BALZAC The Lily in the Valley
POLINA BARSKOVA Living Pictures
ROSALIND BELBEN The Limit
HENRI BOSCO The Child and the River
ANDRÉ BRETON Nadja
DINO BUZZATI The Betwitched Bourgeois: Fifty Stories
CRISTINA CAMPO The Unforgivable and Other Writings
CAMILO JOSÉ CELA The Hive
EILEEN CHANG Written on Water
FRANÇOIS-RENÉ DE CHATEAUBRIAND Memoirs from Beyond the Grave, 1800–1815
AMIT CHAUDHURI Afternoon Raag
LUCILLE CLIFTON Generations: A Memoir
COLETTE Chéri *and* The End of Chéri
ANTONIO DI BENEDETTO The Suicides
JEAN ECHENOZ Command Performance
MICHAEL EDWARDS The Bible and Poetry
BEPPE FENOGLIO A Private Affair
GUSTAVE FLAUBERT The Letters of Gustave Flaubert
BENITO PÉREZ GÁLDOS Miaow
MAVIS GALLANT The Uncollected Stories of Mavis Gallant
MARTIN A. HANSEN The Liar
ELIZABETH HARDWICK The Uncollected Essays of Elizabeth Hardwick
GERT HOFMANN Our Philosopher
HENRY JAMES On Writers and Writing
TOVE JANSSON Sun City
WALTER KEMPOWSKI An Ordinary Youth
PAUL LAFARGUE The Right to Be Lazy
JEAN-PATRICK MANCHETTE Skeletons in the Closet
JOHN McGAHERN The Pornographer
EUGENIO MONTALE Butterfly of Dinard
AUGUSTO MONTERROSO The Rest is Silence
ELSA MORANTE Lies and Sorcery
PIER PAOLO PASOLINI Theorem
DOUGLAS J. PENICK The Oceans of Cruelty: Twenty-Five Tales of a Corpse-Spirit, a Retelling
HENRIK PONTOPPIDAN A Fortunate Man
RUMI Water; translated by Haleh Liza Gafori
JONATHAN SCHELL The Village of Ben Suc
ANTON SHAMMAS Arabesques
CLAUDE SIMON The Flanders Road
WILLIAM GARDNER SMITH The Stone Face
VLADIMIR SOROKIN Blue Lard
ITALO SVEVO A Very Old Man
SUSAN TAUBES Lament for Julia
TEFFI Other Worlds: Peasants, Pilgrims, Spirits, Saints
YŪKO TSUSHIMA Woman Running in the Mountains
LISA TUTTLE My Death
PAUL VALÉRY Monsieur Teste
ROBERT WALSER Little Snow Landscape
MARKUS WERNER The Frog in the Throat
XI XI Mourning a Breast